the summer of hammers & angels

the summer of hammers & angels

Shannon Wiersbitzky

namelos
South Hampton, New Hampshire

Library of Congress Control Number: 2011925043

ISBN 978-1-60898-111-3 (hardcover : alk. paper)
ISBN 978-1-60898-112-0 (pbk. : alk. paper)
ISBN 978-1-60898-113-7 (ebk.)

namelos
www.namelos.com

*For Grandma, who would have felt
right at home in Tucker's Ferry*

Contents

1 Tucker's Ferry

Most folks have never seen an angel.

I know, because I've asked them.

"Nope," or "Not yet," is how they usually answer.

Of course Tommy Parker from my class said, "Huh? How could I see an angel? I'm not dead, Delia."

Tommy is dense as a stump. He wouldn't know an angel if one came up and kicked him in the butt, which of course an angel would never do.

I asked Miss Martha at the post office too. "Maybe someday, Delia, God willing."

God does a lot of willing in Tucker's Ferry, West Virginia.

What with all the faith people put in God around here, it's sort of surprising that they've never seen an angel. You'd think it would be the religious folks who'd see an angel first.

Not someone normal.

Not someone like me.

Before last summer I didn't think about God or angels much, at least not officially. Mostly it was on the big days, like Easter and Christmas, because on the big days we went to church.

Mama wasn't fond of church. I don't know why. She did send me to Vacation Bible School, though. Everyone I knew was there. Kids from Tucker's Ferry didn't go to summer camp.

I liked that week of Bible school. Mornings always started

off with a song. Our teacher, Miss Jackson, taught us hand movements to match the words. Usually we looked like we were trying to flag down a bus.

We went outside when Miss Jackson needed a break. She'd give us a ball or a Frisbee, then sit down on a weathered bench in the shade and watch us play. The game I liked most was kickball. That ball flew like a rocket when I kicked it in exactly the right spot.

Miss Jackson was fond of art projects too. Last year we each painted a ceramic Jesus—or his head and shoulders, anyway. He was about the size of a coffee mug. The other kids gave him long brown hair, a brown beard, and creamy white skin, exactly the way he looks in those color pictures in the Children's Bible. But inspiration was flowing in me that day, and I painted him all sorts of colors, making sure every speck of plain ceramic was covered.

When she saw it, Miss Jackson drew her mouth together in a frown like someone had dropped a brick on her foot. "Delia," she said, "Jesus didn't have rainbow stripes."

I held him high for everyone to see and told her what we'd been taught, that Jesus was all about love and light and that when I thought about those things I thought about rainbows. Miss Jackson didn't give us any more ceramics after that.

Mama thought my Jesus was great. "Now *that* is one happy-looking savior."

We set him on the table by our front door and got into the habit of giving him a little pat as we left the house to get groceries or go to school. Like a good-luck charm. The paint on his head is starting to wear thin now. My little Jesus is going bald.

At Bible school we also sang songs and listened to stories. I love stories.

Take, for instance, the story of Jonah and the whale. We heard that one every year.

Imagine getting swallowed up by a whale. I mean, really!

A whale's belly cannot be a wonderful-smelling place, but Jonah sat there twiddling his thumbs, covered in whale spit and slime. Then God told that whale to take Jonah to the town of Nineveh and toss him right out on the sandy beach.

Throw-up doesn't smell like perfume, so Jonah must have been one stinky guy. I bet he prayed real hard after that and did whatever God told him.

It was probably like getting a spanking. For a few days you follow all the rules, afraid of it happening again. But eventually you go back to doing all the same bad things you did that earned you the spanking in the first place, and praying you don't get caught.

According to Mama, praying is no different than wishing to someone specific. "And wishing doesn't get you anywhere," she says. "Only way to get what you want is through hard work."

Mama is the hardest-working person I know. Since we don't have everything we want, I guess even hard work takes time to pay off. Praying seems like it might be faster.

Directly across from the only stoplight in town is CJ's Diner. That's where Mama works. The diner is always busy. Sometimes people stand in a long snaky line, from the front steps past the newspaper machines and halfway around the parking lot, waiting for tables to clear so they can get in and sit down.

Folks might not be thinking about food, might not even be hungry, but then the light turns red. They sit there, the smell of sizzling bacon and buttermilk biscuits or fresh-grilled hamburgers and fried onions pouring through their windows. People can't help themselves. They have to stop.

I'm not certain, but maybe my meeting angels was like folks stopping at that diner. I didn't mean to do it. I wasn't planning on it. But in the end, I really didn't have much of a choice.

2 The Knock

I woke up on Friday with that smiley feeling you get when you had a good time the night before. Outside my window the cicadas were already singing, which meant three things: hot, hot, and hot. Lying there, wearing pajama shorts and shirt, I scratched the mosquito bites that had welted up on my arms and legs during the night. The mosquitoes were always sneaking in through the torn window screens while I slept, snacking on anything that hung out past the sheets. All summer I itched.

I leaned over the side of the bed, my boring brown curls hanging around my face, and there were my brand-new sandals. Coffee-colored leather straps crisscrossing in front, with pink crystals on top. The kind of shoes you don't see very often in Tucker's Ferry, except maybe at school dances. I couldn't wait to show them to Mae.

Mama never bought me anything I didn't really, really need, but there was a special deal that week at Marvin's Shoes. Buy two for the price of one. I really, really needed new sneakers, and the sandals were like ordering a scoop of vanilla and getting hot fudge for free.

I was still admiring my new shoes and scratching my ankle when I heard Mama yell from the kitchen, "Gather up all your dirty clothes, Delia. It's laundry day."

Laundry wasn't topping my list of fun things to do on Mama's day off, but I didn't figure I was going to get a say one way or the other. At least it meant a trip into town, and a doughnut for breakfast. The Grey family runs a bakery next door to the Speedi-King Laundromat. Mama and I stopped to get one almost every time we passed by, as the scent of fresh-baked doughnuts is near impossible to resist.

The best thing about laundry day was relaxing on the bench outside the bakery while our clothes were washing. Maybe I shouldn't admit it, but I liked Mama best when she was eating doughnuts. As we sat there together, our fingers sticky sweet, watching the cars drive by, things felt easy. Mama didn't worry about bills or complain about her feet, she was simply Mama. More like a friend, really.

At the Speedi-King we loaded our whites and darks into separate machines and jammed in all the quarters (which was the most fun part), then walked over to Grey's Bakery to wait out the wash, rinse, and spin. They had a whole tray of cream-filled doughnuts. My favorite.

"Fresh from the fryer," said Mrs. Grey, wrapping one up for me.

Mrs. Grey always wore a tie-dyed T-shirt, even though she's a grandma. She reminded me of my good-luck Rainbow Jesus, full of color and life.

Mama chose a peanut-crusted doughnut, and we sat down on the bench outside. A girl from school walked past. Her outfit was new, I could tell. It had that smooth, unwrinkled look that never comes back once something gets washed, not even if you iron it. Most of my clothes came from rummages, which meant they had years of wrinkles built right in.

"Hi, Delia," she said, her voice as crisp as the creases in her pleats.

"Hi, Sarah," I mumbled, my mouth half full of cream and pastry.

I was glad Mama and I were sitting on the bench directly in front of the bakery. I bet Sarah and her mom never had to use the Laundromat.

After the doughnuts were gone, we moved the heavy, wet clothes to the dryers. I sat on an empty washer and watched our clothes spin round and round.

Even though we propped the door open with a rock, the Speedi-King had that dog-days-of-summer feel, hot and humid enough to make a toothpick wilt. Sweat dripped from my forehead. Mama's shirt was sticky wet across her back.

We played rock-paper-scissors. Mama tried to play and read one of those tabloid magazines at the same time. The articles about alien babies and end-of-the-world signs must have been super-interesting, because she managed to lose every round. It's no fun beating someone when they're not even trying.

As soon as the dryers beeped, Mama loaded up our baskets, tossed the magazines on top, and headed for the door.

Our house wasn't much cooler than the Laundromat, and the air felt as heavy as a wet blanket. We pointed all our downstairs fans toward the living room. Then we sat down to fold.

We'd gotten through half of our colored basket when there was a knock on the door. Mama and I stared at each other. We didn't get many visitors, except for Mae and the Jehovahs.

When I opened the door there was a man on the porch wearing a loose-fitting suit. He was glancing around, paying particular attention to the white plastic swans perched on the corners. The swans were meant to be full of flowers, but ours grew weeds best. Mama used them mainly to hold down the outdoor carpet that was always curling up like it wanted to escape.

The man frowned at me and cleared his throat. His neck was thin—too thin, it seemed to me, to hold up his extra-large head. And he had these big ears that stuck out, like they were real interested in hearing what you had to say. "I need to speak to your mother, please."

I knew right away this was trouble. He had an official sound to him, like one of those bill collectors who had visited in the past. We weren't fond of bill collectors.

"What can I do for you?" Mama asked. She stepped up next to me so she could see out the door.

"Mrs. Burns," said the man. "I'm a home inspector representing the county." He handed Mama a small white card. "We've received word of numerous health and safety violations with homes in this area. Which is why I'm here."

Mama stared at that man, her eyes getting smaller as he spoke. "What does any of that have to do with me?" Her voice was stone hard.

The inspector gave Mama one of those I'm-so-much-smarter-than-you expressions. A fake smile bent the corners of his mouth. I hated him immediately.

"It means I've come to inspect your home. If there are problems that make it unsafe or unsuitable for living"—he stared at the exact spot on the porch where the carpet covered a hole—"then I'm afraid there will be serious consequences."

"What kind of serious consequences?"

The inspector cleared his throat, his eyes pointed at me.

Mama followed his gaze. "Whatever you have to say, you can say it in front of Delia."

The air was so tight I thought it might snap.

"Fine," said the inspector. "If you fail the inspection, your house will be condemned."

You could have knocked me over with a corn flake when he said that. I glanced at Mama, then the man, then back at Mama again.

"Go to your room, Delia."

While Mama let him in I gathered up the rest of the laundry and tore to my room, avoiding the stairs where the steps were loose. We'd given them a good dose of school glue, but by the looks of it, the school glue hadn't done the trick.

In my room I lay down with my ear against the crack in the floor so I could hear what was going on downstairs. One good thing about having an old house was that it was hard for Mama to keep secrets.

"What right do you have to tell me what to do?" said Mama.

I could picture Mama, hands on her hips, eyes blazing, ready to fight. The inspector said something about looking out for my safety.

"All I ever think about is Delia," said Mama.

They must have started walking around then because their voices began fading in and out. I sat up and folded laundry again, my back against the wall. Every now and then I caught more words. Words like *repairs* and *deadline*, *state law*, and *demolition*.

There certainly were lots of broken things in the house, but, to my way of thinking, none of them mattered much. The toilet didn't work so well, the roof dipped in the middle as if something heavy had sat there once, and when it rained, there was a leak in the kitchen. The good thing about the leak was that it was directly over the sink. If you have a leak, that's about as perfect a spot for one as any.

When I heard them come upstairs I pushed the laundry aside and yanked the comforter over my bed, trying to make the room a bit more presentable. School papers were stacked in an uneven tower in the corner. The dresser top was cluttered with brushes, barrettes, and candy wrappers.

Mama took that inspector to her room first, then the bathroom in the middle of the hall. When he started toward my room I held my breath.

"No need to go in there," said Mama. "You won't find anything you haven't noted already."

I heaved a big sigh and slumped onto the bed.

It wasn't but a few minutes later that the front door slammed. I was pulling a comb through my curls, trying to straighten them. When I looked out my window the inspector was standing by his car making notes on a pad of paper. He glanced up and caught me staring. I gave him my meanest glare, then went downstairs to find Mama.

3 The Storm

On Saturday, Mama's foul mood filled up the house. I opened the front door to get some air through the screen, but Mama pulled it tight and turned the lock.

"Never know what might get in," she said.

I kept an eye out for the inspector's car all day, but it never came. Mama sat on the worn plaid couch with the business card he'd given her. She read it over and over, clutching it, almost tearing it, not saying a word, her anger brewing like real strong tea. It was as if she was hearing his words again every time she looked at it.

With a ragged washcloth in one hand and a can of lemon polish in the other, I buffed and rubbed all around Mama the entire morning, waxing every piece of furniture we had, even though most of it was plastic. The smell of lemony goodness always made me feel better, and I was hoping it might improve Mama's temper.

After lunch I finally got up the nerve to ask her a question. "Mama, is the inspector coming back?"

"Yes," was all she said. Then she started crying.

I guess God thought she needed some company because it started raining at that very same moment. Raindrops smacked the roof of the front porch. I waited, knowing those drops would run along the cracks in the brick and find their way in. Then *plunk, plunk, plunk,* the leak in the kitchen began to splish in the sink.

I counted splishes for a while. When I got to forty-two a door slammed upstairs. I checked the couch—Mama was gone. She'd left me there with only the leak for company.

At times like that it sure would have been nice to have a sister, a brother even, to help use up all that empty space.

Mama once told me that babies choose their families. If that's true, then I guess I didn't look around very long. When I was a baby spirit, flying up there in heaven with the angels, I must have gotten too excited and hasty in my picking, because I've got the smallest family of anyone I know—it's only Mama and me. I don't even have one cousin. My best friend Mae has a bushel.

Even with the TV on, I could hear Mama crying, her voice rising up every now and then in a loud wail. The storm matched her step by step, thunder clapping, lightning striking, and rain pouring in thick sheets outside the front picture window. It was a mighty fierce storm.

When my stomach started growling I set a pot of water on the stove to boil and cooked myself some macaroni and cheese from a box. The ceiling was damp all around that drip. Peeling paint curled up along the edges of the water stain, which grew wider as I watched.

Since Mama wasn't there to see, I crushed a handful of potato chips on top of my noodles, grabbed a grape pop, and sat back down in front of the TV. Then I opened Mama's tabloid magazine and read about those alien babies.

The storm was still howling when I went to bed. Strange as it sounds, I love sleeping during storms. Listening to the wind and the rain and the anger of the world while I'm tucked under my blankets makes me feel cozy and safe.

I heard Mama walk down the hall to the bathroom once, the floor complaining the entire way. The sound of her footsteps pulled me from sleep.

Later that night I woke up in a rush, my breath coming in spurts like I'd been playing a game of tag. I breathed deep and coughed, my throat suddenly scratchy. The air smelled like burnt toast.

It was supposed to be dark, but the lightning and thunder were putting on a show and every few seconds the entire house lit up. When the thunder boomed, it felt as if we were inside a drum.

I rushed from my room but didn't get more than a few steps. Rough pieces of wood lay on the floor alongside chunks of ceiling. I sidestepped them while trying to avoid the rain that was pouring in. I wasn't sure if it was God or those aliens, but someone had taken a giant can opener and cut a hole in our roof to see what was inside. From the hallway I could look up through the ceiling and the attic to the roof and the sky beyond. Orange flames licked at the edges of the hole, despite the rain.

"Mama!" I yelled.

My voice was no match for the thunder. Mama didn't answer. Still screaming, I flung open her door and saw her lying crumpled by the window.

"Mama!" I cried, shaking her. "We've got to get out!"

Bits of wall and windowsill lay on and around Mama like a strange summer snow. I screamed again. I put my face close to hers and could feel the faintest of breath.

The burnt smell was even stronger in Mama's room. When I took her hand it was limp. I could see there was a black mark on her palm. I stood behind her, her wrists in mine, and tugged. She didn't move.

I grabbed the phone. Dialed.

9-1-1. 9-1-1. 9-1-1.

There was no sound on the other end and I rattled the phone, trying to get someone to pick up. "Hello!"

The phone was dead.

I stared at Mama, then the door. Mama, the door. Mama. Door.

I raced down the steps and out of the house, looking back only once to see low flames rising from the roof. Water slapped my legs as I ran across the yard and through the tall grass to the closest neighbor we had, the Parkers.

With both fists I pounded on the Parkers' front door. Pounded as fast as my beating heart. Pounded until I thought the door might fall in from me thumping on it. A light came on, shining through the window, and at last I wasn't alone.

The Parkers' phone was working fine. Mr. Parker called the police even as I was telling them about Mama and the rain and the fire.

I ran back to the house with Mr. Parker. It seemed farther away than it was only a few minutes earlier. My eyes went directly to the roof, but the flames hadn't gotten worse. The rain was snuffing them out.

I led Mr. Parker up the stairs, straight to Mama. He felt her wrist and put fingers to her neck. Then he patted her gently on the cheek and called her name, but it was no use.

We could hear the sirens screaming in the night as they made their way to our house. It was strange, terrible music, announcing something sad. The whirling sound seemed to echo forever in the darkness. At last the flashing lights arrived in our driveway.

Paramedics in white and navy rushed in with a stretcher and a wide rectangular box of supplies. A fireman in a yellow slicker and black hat ran past Mama's bedroom door, a fire extinguisher in his hands. I could hear him shouting to someone else, and then there was a whooshing sound. I looked into the hall. The fireman had the extinguisher aimed straight up, covering everything in sight with thick white foam.

Mr. Parker took me to the living room while the paramedics worked. We sat on the edge of the couch and he squeezed my hand. I could feel the rough calluses on his skin.

At that moment, sitting there drenched in the spit and slime of the biggest storm in Tucker's Ferry history, I understood how Jonah must have felt. I began to wonder if God had something big planned for me too.

4 Hot Chocolate

It wasn't until I got to the hospital that I realized I wasn't wearing any shoes. Specks of dirt and weeds and freshly mowed grass clippings were stuck to my legs. I wiped them off as best I could and then tucked my legs under me Indian-style. Mr. Parker patted my hand.

"How long do you think it'll be until we can see Mama?"

"I'll go check."

Mr. Parker stood and crossed the room to where a nurse in colorful scrubs sat behind a counter. A stethoscope was draped over her shoulders and behind her neck. She had a crooked smile, as if one side of her mouth was more tired than the other.

I glanced around the waiting area. A woman lay sleeping across four chairs, her hair a tangled, knotted mess around her face. Another man drank coffee and stared at the ceiling, an open book in his hand. He never turned one page. I wondered how long they'd been waiting.

There was a television mounted in a corner, high on the wall. Colors flickered like a neon sign. It was on some news channel. The sound was down so low that I couldn't hear it.

When Mr. Parker came back, he was holding two cups of hot chocolate. I took one of the cups and sipped it slowly. I don't normally drink hot chocolate in the summer, but that night it was the closest thing to a hug from Mama, so I drank it real slow.

"You'll be able to see her soon," Mr. Parker told me.

"What happened?" I asked him.

"Lightning hit your house. That's what made the hole in the roof and started the fire. Judging from the burns on her hands, the doctors think that when the lightning struck, it somehow hit your mama too. Lightning can do funny things, zigzag all over the place. It must have gone through the wires." He said the last sentence quietly, as if he was talking to himself.

I remembered the black marks I'd seen on Mama's palms. Burns.

Then Mr. Parker gazed at the floor like it was the most interesting thing in the entire world. "Your mama's in a coma. They aren't real sure yet when she'll wake up."

I thought about that. "Lightning usually kills people when it hits them, doesn't it?"

Mr. Parker nodded. "Your mama's real lucky."

Anything strong enough to put a hole through the roof should have been able to kill Mama. But she was still alive. Alive and in the hospital where the doctors and nurses could take care of her. I figured that maybe all her hard work was starting to pay off at last.

Drinking hot chocolate was the last thing I remember about that night. Mr. Parker must have carried me to Mama's room, because when I woke up, stretched out across two cushioned chairs, there she was, lying next to me in a hospital bed. There were beeping machines and a few tubes, but it was still Mama.

I crawled onto the bed and turned onto my side, squeezing myself into the thin sliver of space between Mama and the edge. To keep myself from falling off I draped an arm over her chest and laid my head against her shoulder. Her breath was whisper soft. In. Out. In. Out. I matched my breathing to hers. For a moment I almost believed she was sleeping and that we were back at home, lying on her flowered bedspread. I ran my fingers down her face.

Without even noticing it I moved my right ear directly over Mama's heart. The steady *da-dum, da-dum, da-dum* vibrated in my head. I focused hard on the beat, my eyes closed, whispering along with it. "Wake up, wake up, wake up."

I held Mama tighter and tried to ignore the unfamiliar sounds of the hospital.

A shrill beep kept going off. There was the ping of metal, ripping plastic. I could hear the phone ringing at the nurses' station. An announcement over the intercom asked that a wheelchair be taken to Room 264. In the hall someone was rolling a cart. Its wheels jangled.

"Wake up, Mama. It's me, Delia."

I wondered if she could hear me, wherever she was. I'd heard stories about people being in a coma. Sometimes they could hear what was happening around them the whole time; sometimes they couldn't. Sometimes they woke up quick, and sometimes it took years for them to find their way back.

It might be nice to skip over a day or two, especially one with a big test or anything involving Tommy Parker, but then I'd want to wake up. I'd hate to sleep my whole life away and miss the big things like driving or my first kiss.

Voices in the hall caught my attention. I could hear Mr. Parker.

I climbed from the bed and cracked open the door. He was standing with a nurse. This one was pink from head to toe. Pink flowered scrubs, a pink headband holding back her shiny black hair, even pink rubber shoes. She reminded me of that medicine Mama made me take when my stomach hurt.

"Not sure we have a choice, seeing as Delia doesn't have any relatives that I know of here in Tucker's Ferry. We'll take her home with us."

She made a note on her clipboard. "Thanks, Jack. We'll call you the minute there's a change."

Hearing *Jack* struck me odd. I never knew that was Mr. Parker's first name.

It's strange what your brain thinks about when life is coming up all wrong. Useless things like the fact that Mr. Parker's left shoelace had been undone last night, or that the remote control for Mama's hospital bed had twelve buttons.

I turned from the door and almost leapt to Mama's bed, grabbing her bandaged hand. Things were moving from bad to really terrible.

"Oh, Mama, you've got to wake up or else I'm going to have to live with Tommy Parker. I'll die! I'll wither like Old Red Clancy's corn in October. Oh, please, Mama, wake up!"

5 Packing and Unpacking

Mrs. Parker took me to my house so I could pack my things. I walked through the living room and up the stairs the way I had a million times. This time it was like walking through an empty shell, hollow and cold.

In the hallway it was as if the fireman had painted everything white with that fire extinguisher. I stared up through the hole in the ceiling to the charred rafters in the roof. Someone had covered the hole with plastic during the night, a milky colored plastic that made the sky seem further away than usual.

My room hadn't changed a bit. The closet door was flung wide; drawers were half open. There were hair bands, folded notes from Mae, and an empty tube of lip gloss scattered across my dresser. The folded laundry from Friday still sat in piles on the floor. I stared at it all, not knowing where to begin.

Mrs. Parker chattered the entire time, setting a cardboard box from the IGA on my bed and opening it up.

"Should we start with clothes? That might be the easiest. You'll need shorts and shirts and a few dresses for church. Then we can pack all your toiletries. We can always pop back over too, honey, so we don't need to get everything today."

I did as she said. It was nice having Mrs. Parker there to tell me what to do. My head felt muddled, like it was under water. Into the box went clothes and shoes, a book I'd barely started reading, and a small teddy bear. Mrs. Parker disappeared into the bathroom and then came back with a flowered bag I'd never seen before.

"I packed your toothbrush and floss, a hairbrush, and a few other things." She held up the bag and then added it to the box. "Are we all set, then?"

I did my best to answer, but I could feel my mouth quivering, the tears hot at the corners of my eyes.

When we arrived at the Parkers' house, Mrs. Parker balanced the box on one knee and opened the screen, holding it with a hip.

"Go on in," she said.

I stepped inside and eyed the room, taking in the polished coffee table and the flowered sofa, matching pillows lined up neatly across the back.

The screen door slammed behind her when she walked in, making me jump.

"Follow me," said Mrs. Parker, shifting the box. "I'll show you your room."

As we walked up the creaky stairs I couldn't help but study the wall and all the people there. It seemed like the entire Parker history was framed and on display. I remembered what Mr. Parker said at the hospital when he didn't know I could hear him. I didn't have a family.

"Here we are."

I almost cried when I found out my new room was only a strong spit away from Tommy's.

"You make yourself right at home, Delia. While you're here you're just like kin." Mrs. Parker smiled and gave me a hug. I knew she meant well, but all I could think about was being Tommy Parker's sister. It made me want to curl up and die or barf or both.

I didn't know what else to do, so I started unpacking. Mrs. Parker had cleared a dresser for all my things. Each of the drawers was lined with lavender-scented paper. When I opened them up, it was like standing in a flower shop.

I glared at Tommy every time he walked past, which was pretty often. He seemed to have nothing better to do than torment me. I kept thinking of ways to shut him up. None of them were legal.

"Is that your underwear?" he asked during one trip.

I quickly shoved it all in a drawer. "My underwear is none of your business. Why don't you go bother someone else?"

He stood there smirking. "Know what, Delia Burns? I'm gonna start calling you Bad-Luck Burns. What do you think about that?" He burped—a long, forever-sounding burp that only a disgusting boy with no manners could make. "This is my house. I can stand wherever I want to."

I gritted my teeth and kept putting clothes away. Tommy's eyes bored into my back. I could feel them. But I didn't turn around. I kept right on doing what I was doing.

Mrs. Parker came upstairs as I was placing my last shirts in those perfumed drawers. Having her so close reminded me of Mama. Made it harder to forget why I was there in the first place. I sat at the foot of the bed and she sat down too, the mattress sagging in her direction. She pulled me to her in a sideways hug, then rubbed my back. I closed my eyes, trying to keep the tears from falling, and breathed deep, the soft scent of her perfume, magnolias and lavender, mixing together in my head.

"Don't worry, honey. It'll be all right. You'll see."

We sat there then, not saying a word, me crying quiet as an afternoon rain.

Mrs. Parker let me go and I lay down on the bed, clutching a pillow in my arms. The thin summer quilt was cool against my skin. She stroked my hair over and over. My eyelids grew heavy and I let them fall.

Sleep was the one thing I was good at the first few days after Mama was hurt. I didn't have the energy for anything else. I slept late in the morning, took long naps in the middle of the day, and went to bed early.

Most days a breeze blew the lacy white curtains, and the sweet smell of honeysuckle from the Parkers' backyard would wash over me. Honeysuckle smells warm, like fresh buttered biscuits. When I felt like sleeping that honeysuckle air was as good as a lullaby.

Sometimes when I woke up I could hear Tommy Parker fussing downstairs. "How come Delia gets to lie around all day and I've got to do chores?"

"Tommy," said Mrs. Parker, "you stop your sassing right this instant. Delia needs a few days to find her feet."

Knowing that I was annoying Tommy made me smile. Made me want to stay in bed forever.

6 Best Friends

When Mae finally came to visit, she hugged me tight. She'd heard about the lightning from Miss Martha at the post office. Tucker's Ferry wasn't an easy place to keep secrets.

"I would have come straightaway after the accident but Mrs. Parker and my mom decided to let you rest for a few days." Mae scowled. "What person in their right mind doesn't feel better with their best friend? Answer me that, will you? Grownups can be stupid. That's all I have to say."

Mae was right. Having my best friend there did make me feel better. We sat on the front porch and stared at the cornfield across the street, which belonged to Old Red Clancy. I frowned at Tommy Parker when he made stupid faces at us from the front window. I wished I could make him disappear.

"How's your mama?"

"They told me they'd call if she woke up, but they haven't called yet." I watched an ant crawl along the porch step.

"Were you scared?" asked Mae. She reached out and squeezed my hands.

"Not at first," I answered. "I felt the rain and saw the fire and it was more confusing than scary. But when Mama didn't answer, the fear came at me, baring its teeth and growling, like Old Red Clancy's dog, Rex."

We were quiet then.

I was thinking about Rex. He was a mean mutt. Every time we rode past Old Red's house, if Rex was out, he came running. He'd never bitten anyone, but it wasn't for lack of wanting. If Rex was locked up inside the house, we'd park our bikes by the gate, then walk alongside the chain-link fence, dragging sticks along the metal. That always made Rex howl.

We stopped at Old Red's even knowing we might run into him and his dog. There was only one front yard in Tucker's Ferry like Old Red's. He had burnt-orange lilies that reminded me of angry Halloween jack-o'-lanterns, and others that were blood red. There were blossoms gray as a stormy sky, even purple ones that in the sun shone black.

Except for a few steppingstones near the gate, every bit of earth we could see was growing. There were bees and hummingbirds too, their wings a blur from beating so fast. Like they were in a hurry to get in and get out. Seeing that garden should have been like peeking into heaven. But it was more like a prison of flowers.

"Do you believe in heaven?" I asked, leaning back on the porch.

Mae thought for a moment, her chin in her hands. She never got to answer me because at that exact moment a car drove up the road. It was driving faster than most cars did, its tires spitting loose bits of rock and a plume of dust trailing behind. You could have pushed me over with a dandelion puff when I saw the driver.

It was the inspector.

Normally there isn't much I don't remember. What with the lightning, the hospital, Mama, and the pain of moving right across the hallway from Tommy Parker, though, I'd forgotten about that inspector.

"Who is that?"

I grabbed Mae by the arm and yanked her down. "Shhh."

Mae and I moved spy style, crouching and sneaking down four empty lots, from the Parkers' house to my own, where the inspector was waiting on the front porch. Standing there with his smug smile overtop of his pencil neck. He nudged one of the white swans with the toe of his dull leather shoe. I decided I didn't hate him as much as broccoli. I hated him as much as stewed spinach, which was even worse.

A broad oak gave us camouflage and we flattened ourselves against the scratchy bark, peeking out to see what he was doing, hoping he couldn't see us. The inspector rapped on the front door, then peered in the front window, his hand over his eyes. He had on that same crumpled suit. It was as if he was wearing his daddy's clothes. When we didn't answer the door he stepped into the yard and stared up at the roof, which had a new hole in it since the last time he visited.

"Do you know him?" asked Mae.

I answered in a hushed tone. "It's the county inspector."

"What's a county inspector doing at your house?"

"He came the day the lightning struck. Said Mama had to fix up the house or they'd make us move."

Mae's mouth hung open. "*What*?"

"Shhh!"

Mae isn't very good at keeping quiet. She's the worst whisperer in all of Tucker's Ferry.

I peeked around the tree again to see if the inspector had heard us. With his elephant ears, I figured he could hear a gnat hiccup. But that inspector didn't even glance in our direction. He shoved a white envelope between the screen and the front door and then turned toward his car. As he walked past, he reached up and backhanded our rusty wind chimes.

We waited for him to drive off, then walked to the front porch. I pulled the envelope from the door and tore it open. I probably shouldn't have done that, seeing as it was addressed to Mama. At that moment, though, I got the feeling that the future of the Burns women was up to me.

7 The List

The hospital was the way I remembered it—cold. I thought about getting some more of that hot chocolate.

Mama hadn't changed. With her long blond hair loose around her face, watching her was like staring at a painting of an angel, the kind they have in museums behind red velvet ropes. It was hard to believe she was sick. I didn't know if being in a coma was sick like having pneumonia or cancer, but it wasn't normal, that was for sure.

A framed picture of sunflowers hung on the wall near the bed. Mama loved sunflowers. To her mind, they were the hardest-working flower of them all.

"Look how tall they have to grow," Mama used to say, "before they can bloom."

I thought her loving them had to do with my daddy. Mama hardly ever talked about him, except to say that he was great at two things: making promises and breaking them. I asked her once how they met. Mama said he'd walked straight over to her, in front of all her friends, and given her a sunflower. Told her they were as bright as her smile.

Old Red Clancy grew sunflowers in his garden every summer. They were always taller than me, but sometimes they were even taller than Mama.

"Hi, Mama. It's Delia." I shoved the chair next to her bed and held her hand. It was still bandaged with white gauze and felt puffy, as if Mama was wearing a mitten.

I got directly to the point. "Mama, you've got to wake up. Tommy Parker says he's going to hang my underwear from the flagpole at school in September. He might be prying in my dresser this very instant. He burps all the time too, like he's got some sort of medical condition. Really, I'm not making it up!"

Mama listened. At least it felt that way to me.

"The inspector came back. He left some papers."

I pulled the folded pages from my backpack. There was an official stamp at the top and a date for the next inspection. With my fingers I counted days, trying to remember which months had thirty and which had thirty-one. Then I counted a second time, just to be sure.

"We have nineteen days, Mama."

The papers said our house needed loads of fixing. The inspector had listed each problem on a separate line next to an empty square that I guess we were supposed to check off when we'd taken care of it. An official to-do list. I read Mama the lines, one by one.

The problems went on and on and on.

When I was finished, I sat there in the silence with Mama, staring at the pages and listening to the beeping machines.

After a while that beeping sounded worse than nails on a blackboard. I grabbed my stuff and went to the hospital cafeteria.

"A hot chocolate, please."

"My favorite," said the woman behind the counter. The expression on her wrinkled face reminded me of summer. Like homemade ice cream and half-melted marshmallows. "You here visiting someone, dear?"

I nodded. "My mama."

The woman wiped her hands on her apron, which was stretched tight around her middle. She sprayed an extra-tall swirl of whipped cream on the top and handed it to me. "I'm Miss Beatrice. This is my kitchen. If you ever get hungry while you're visiting your mama, you come here, understand?"

Judging from the smells in the cafeteria, Miss Beatrice knew how to cook.

I sat by myself in a booth at the corner of the room, taking tiny sips of hot chocolate and licking whipped cream off my upper lip. From there I could see the register, the other tables, and the food line, where Miss Beatrice filled plates and talked to customers. In between sips I fiddled with the salt and pepper shakers and counted packets of jam that were stacked in a black plastic holder. It held twelve altogether. There were eleven strawberry and one orange marmalade.

I was about halfway through my drink when I heard Miss Beatrice yell.

"Dad blame it!" she said, standing next to the hot-chocolate machine. She pressed the button on the front four or five times, the way I did sometimes when I was trying to get a stoplight to change faster so I could walk across the street. Even from where I was sitting I could hear the sickly whine of the motor or whatever it was inside.

Miss Beatrice disappeared through a swinging door that went to the kitchen. I stared at the square window and finished my whipped cream. The hot chocolate had cooled enough so I could take bigger swallows.

There was clanging and cussing and then Miss Beatrice

pushed through the door like a cowboy in an Old West saloon. In her right hand she held a thick wooden mallet, the kind used to pound meat. She went straight over to that broken machine and started clanging on the heavy pipes that wound in circles around the back. I wasn't sure if she was meaning to fix it or put it out of its misery.

I pulled out the inspector's papers, carefully pressing the edges until they lay almost flat on the table. One at a time I reread each problem.

"That's right!" shouted Miss Beatrice, waving her mallet. "You'd better start working or I'll hit you some more."

The machine began gurgling, spitting out hot chocolate in fits. Miss Beatrice fiddled with the pipes on the back, turning dials and adjusting knobs.

Suddenly it hit me. I swallowed the last of my hot chocolate even as I was climbing out of the booth, and then started running.

"Mama," I said, huffing from taking the stairs two at a time and racing through the long hallway, "I've got a plan."

A flood of ideas rushed through my mind as I paced around Mama's room, which suddenly seemed too small. It took four big steps to get from one wall to the other, and three steps to move from the window to the door. When I hit an edge I turned like a soldier, pivoting in place and heading back the other direction.

Anyone walking past must have thought I was crazy, moving through the room like a caged lion, talking to myself, with Mama lying silent in the bed.

"A hammer, nails, a saw, measuring tape, wood."

On the way home I figured I'd stop at the library. I'd

find one of those "how-to" books on home repair. They had a how-to book for everything else. How to catch a fish or paint a picture, fix a car or build a hot-air balloon. What I needed to learn was a lot less tricky than building a hot-air balloon. At least I thought so.

I kissed Mama goodbye. The first thing I needed to do was talk to Mae.

8 A Good Whupping

Mae lived in an apartment in town, above Carmine's Canine Salon. Every day after the dogs had their anti-flea baths and the blow dryers got going, all that hot, damp air rose straight up through the ceiling. Mae's house became an oven, an oven that smelled like wet dog.

Carmine's had already started the drying process when I arrived. Even though the window air conditioner was running full steam in the living room, it was still sweltering. Mae and I sat down on the cool kitchen linoleum and leaned against the cabinets. Sweat beaded on our foreheads.

"I'm going to fix the house," I said.

"What?" Mae's eyebrows arched like I'd told her I was planning to kill Santa Claus.

My lips tight, I nodded.

"Delia, you don't know anything about fixing houses."

I had to give her that. "I may not, but I'm good at figuring things out. How hard can it be?"

Mae shrugged. "So what do you need?" Mae knew I was asking without even asking. Sometimes best friends can read your mind like that.

"A hammer."

There weren't any tools at my house. If it couldn't be fixed with the turn of a butter knife, a piece of tape, or school glue, Mama would sigh and say, "We'll get to that one of these days, Delia."

One of these days never came. Most repairs required some sort of planning ahead, which wasn't Mama's strong suit. Mama was more of a take-life-as-it-comes kind of person.

"I can give you my daddy's hammer." Mae jumped up off the floor. "Mom says the only thing his tools are good for anyway is collecting dust, so you might as well use it."

With the list in my backpack, the hammer in my hand, and Mae yapping up a storm, we went to my house, kicking rocks to each other along the way. She reminded me of Mrs. Parker those first few days, drowning out every inch of quiet so I wouldn't think about Mama.

"What do you want to fix first? Do you have nails? Won't you need to buy wood or paint? Where will you get the money?"

I kept on walking, my eyes fixed straight ahead of me. I didn't have all the answers yet, and I was afraid that Mae's questions would make me lose my nerve if I listened to them.

The house key hung from my neck on a strand of fuzzy blue yarn. I pulled it off, slid it into the crooked metal lock, and opened the front door. Mae and I patted my Rainbow Jesus as we walked in. The Parkers' house did not have a bald Jesus in the front entrance. I'd missed him.

There was a pen in the kitchen from Grey's Bakery—printed with their name and address in case you forgot where they were. I grabbed it and Mae and I went room to room, searching for all the problems that inspector had written down.

It didn't take us long to find them. There were torn screens and missing floorboards. Leaky patches of ceiling, which meant leaky patches of roof or cracks in the brick (according to the papers). Holes in walls that had been there for as long as I remembered, pipes that dripped and wires that hung out from places they weren't supposed to.

We were still standing in the living room when I saw Tommy Parker walk across the yard. I pulled Mae to the floor.

"Don't say anything!" I whispered. The front door was standing wide open, and I knew that if Mae said even one word aloud, Tommy would be on us like stickon glue.

"What is it?" said Mae in a much louder whisper than mine. I could see Tommy Parker cock his head in our direction as if he heard something but wasn't sure where it came from.

"Shush!" I pleaded under my breath, my eyes going wide in desperation. "Tommy Parker is outside."

Mae turned quickly to look and stubbed her toe on one of the loose floorboards. "Ow!" she cried.

I shook my head as Tommy Parker bounded up the porch steps and pulled open the screen door. Mae's poor whispering skills had done us in again.

"What are you guys doing?" asked Tommy, coming right on in.

"Nothing," I said. I gave him my best get-lost-or-else stare. It didn't bother him one bit. "Mae and I were by ourselves and didn't invite you, if you hadn't noticed."

"My mom wanted me to come find you. Supper is almost ready." Tommy glanced around the room. I knew he was comparing the worn plaid couch and the plastic tables to the plumped and polished furniture at his house. "You-all shouldn't be here alone, you know. Mama wouldn't like it at all if I told her."

"Don't you threaten me, Tommy Parker," I said, shaking a fist at him. I was still clutching the papers, so they shook at him too. Tommy reached over and snatched them.

"Hey!" I yelled. "Give those back. They're mine."

Tommy turned away from me, holding the papers high in the air. "Whatever they are, they're mine now, Delia. If you want them back you'd best let me be."

Watching him read through all those problems made me feel twisted inside. I wanted to punch him right smack under his pale white chin. Tommy's house was perfect. Mr. Parker tinkered all the time, fixing loose doorknobs and greasing hinges. And Mrs. Parker was always running the sweeper or dusting or baking so that the whole house smelled like it had come fresh out of the oven and was about to win a blue ribbon at the state fair.

"You girls won't be able to do any of this, you know. I bet you couldn't fix even one dang thing on here." He was holding out the papers for me to take back. I grabbed them and shoved them in my pack.

"Can too," I answered, holding my balled fists at my side.

"Cannot." Tommy's nose was tilted up in an I'm-right-and-you're-wrong sort of way. Then his eyes flashed and he smiled sweet as honey. "Ask me real nice, though, and I might help you."

"What?" I was sure I'd heard him wrong. Sure that Tommy was up to his usual no good.

"My grandpa taught me all about working with wood. I can drive a nail in with only three hits. Daddy can do it with one, but I'm not as strong as him. Yet."

"What else can you do?"

"I know how to measure and saw and make nail holes disappear, and I can miter corners, which is really tricky."

I'd never heard of mitered corners, but I wasn't about to let Tommy know. Plus, it sounded like it might be kind of important. I glanced at Mae, who until now had been stretched out with her eyes closed on the patched sofa, not saying anything at all. She shrugged.

"All right," I said. "But only because you know how to miter."

"Ask me real nice," said Tommy. He stood with his arms crossed, one foot tapping on the floor.

"You make me so mad, Tommy Parker!" I stomped out the door and stood on the front porch. That boy needed a good whupping. With a willow branch. A thin one that would sting real bad.

The white plastic swan on the corner gave me a sad face. Even she knew Tommy was right. With a deep breath I marched back in and walked right up to him, our noses only a few inches apart.

"I'd appreciate it if you'd help fix the house, Tommy." My words were hard and cold.

Tommy's face lit up like a firefly on a hot August night. Then he nodded and stared at his shoes like it was no big deal.

"Meet back here tomorrow morning and we'll get started," I said. I wanted to make sure Tommy knew who was really in charge.

Before we ate dinner that night, the Parkers prayed. They all reached out their hands to one another, making a circle around the entire table. I had to hold Tommy Parker's hand. Actually, I held on to one fingertip and tried to pretend we weren't touching. I still wanted to smack him upside the head, but I smiled instead, since we were about ready to pray and all.

"Lord, bless this food which we are about to receive. Watch over Cassie Burns and her daughter, Delia."

Then Tommy said, "Amen."

As soon as the prayer was officially over, I dropped Tommy's fingertip like it was a dead fish. Mrs. Parker gave my other hand a little squeeze, then let it go.

After dinner was cleaned up, everyone went out to sit on the front porch. Mrs. Parker brought a big basket of green beans for us to string. If I ignored Mr. Parker and Tommy, I could almost imagine that it was me and Mama sitting there eating doughnuts while our laundry was in the machines at the Speedi-King. That was pretty much the only time Mama ever sat and talked.

Mrs. Parker hardly ever seemed to be in a hurry. She'd sip her coffee and watch the sun come up over Old Red Clancy's corn as if that sunrise was the most important thing in the world. We'd sit together and watch the hummingbirds flit from flower to flower, drinking the nectar without even slowing down.

I heard once that hummingbirds can't stop flying for even a minute or they'll die. I wasn't sure if that was true or not, but I'd never seen one sitting anywhere taking a break. They were sort of like Mama, always busy, always in a hurry.

"What's your favorite kind of doughnut?" I asked Mrs. Parker. I tossed another bean into her good pile.

"Ooh, that's a tough one. Let me think."

She snapped a bean in half, pulling the string down one side and up the other.

"I like the powdered sugar ones, but I think my favorite are the cream filled."

I slapped my thigh, breaking the bean in my hand. "That's my favorite too!"

Mr. Parker said he liked chocolate glazed best, and Tommy's favorite was jelly. That figured. I hated jelly doughnuts.

9 Hammers and Nails

I've noticed that houses take on the personality of the people who live in them. I'm not sure how it happens, but they become alive in some way, as if they have their own spirit. Take the Parkers' house. With its neatly trimmed grass and tidy patches of flowers along the front porch, it was cheerful and friendly, just like Mrs. Parker. Then there was Old Red Clancy's house—a locked metal fence trapping a jungle of creeping ivies, weeds, and thorny roses, and a guard dog, Rex, better than any Keep Out sign, snarling at any bird, butterfly, or girl who might try to sneak in.

Whatever spirit had lived in our house was long gone. I could tell as I walked up the front steps the next day. The house had an empty feeling about it, and it wasn't only because we weren't living there anymore. I bet that spirit got sucked up by the storm when the lightning struck. I wondered if it was swirling around the clouds, keeping an eye out for Tucker's Ferry.

As I walked across the front porch I rang the chimes. The notes were dull and flat and fell quickly in the bright morning sun. I sat down on the corner, the outdoor carpet pricking my skin. Then I pulled the thin good-for-nothing weeds from the swans and tossed them to the ground. Those white swans needed bright red flowers. Flowers with thick green stems, wide leaves, and blooms that would stand up tall and proud, no matter what kind of storm passed over. Old Red had flowers like that in his garden. I knew he wouldn't give me any, though, even if I asked.

I unlocked the front door and made my way to the kitchen. Using magnets, I hung each page from that stupid inspector on the refrigerator. By now, from all that carrying around, the papers were even more creased and rumpled. I tried to flatten them again, smoothing them out with my hand as if I was ironing, but it didn't do much good.

When Mae and Tommy showed up, I was already hard at work on the front porch.

"You pulling off all that carpet?" asked Tommy.

I rolled my eyes. "What's it look like?" I mean, really! Half the carpeting was already off the porch, rolled and clumped in piles. Sometimes I wondered how Tommy Parker managed to tie his shoes. "I wanted to start with something easy. The inspector said the rotted wood under the carpet is a health hazard. Which is stupid, because everyone around here knows which spots to avoid."

Tommy and Mae bent over next to me and we all tugged the carpet together. It was even easier with the three of us. When we got to the end of the porch we jumped off and gave it a good yank. The whole piece fell at our feet in a tired heap. With Tommy and me at the ends and Mae in the middle, we lugged it to the edge of the road and dumped it.

"Will the garbage men take it?" asked Mae.

I stood there with sweat rolling down my face, fanning myself. "I sure hope so."

We walked back through the yard and stared at the porch. It didn't look quite as I expected. Instead of the worn green outdoor carpet curling up on the corners and bunching in the middle, now there was cracked, dry wood. There were open holes where the planks had worn through or broken at some point, and places where the nails had come loose, which made the wood seesaw whenever someone stepped on it.

Mae put an arm around me. "We'll fix it, Delia. It's only Friday, after all. How many days do we have left?"

"Seventeen." I knew I needed to keep close count.

I closed my eyes and stood there for a moment. I could see what the front porch wanted to be. Could see it clear as day. Dark wooden planks with freshly painted white railings all around, flowerpots with color spilling over the edge. Shiny black wicker stuffed with peach cushions. A place where I could sit and read, or eat doughnuts and talk with Mama.

When I opened my eyes, Tommy Parker was standing directly in front of me. He was holding two hammers and had a strange expression on his face. As if he knew a secret that Mae and I didn't.

"It isn't as bad as it looks."

My eyebrows must have shot straight to heaven.

"No, really," he said. "My grandaddy fixed up his porch once and it was in worse shape than this." He handed me a hammer, then knelt down and ran one hand over the wood. "We need to check each nail. Super-loose—pull it out and put in a new one. Sorta loose—try nailing it back in. You'll feel if it grabs the wood or not. All the others, give them a whack for good measure."

It was hard to believe that I was standing there with a hammer and taking instructions from Tommy Parker. My first instinct was to give him a good whack. Seeing as he was the only one who knew what to do, though, I followed orders.

"We only have two hammers," Mae said, pouting.

I wasn't about to remind her that the hammer I had was hers. Hitting nails was something I'd been waiting for.

Tommy set a chipped Marshall University mug crammed with nails by the front door so we could both reach it.

"Come on, Mae," I said. "Let's you and me work together."

Mae trudged over and we went to the left side of the house while Tommy went opposite. There were maybe a million boards between us. Each one had nails as far as the eye could see, which meant I wasn't sure we'd ever finish. I tried to focus on one board and not think about the rest.

As I hammered I realized that Tommy was right. It wasn't as bad as it looked. The front porch had a thick layer of dirt from sitting under the carpet, but that would wash off.

"Are we done yet?" Mae handed me a nail. We were on our second board. Mae had the patience of a flea. I knew she needed a different job.

"Mae, go in the kitchen and get a bucket of soapy water. There's a scrub brush under the sink. Then you can give the porch a wash."

She thought for a second, her mouth scrunched up. "Okay."

Mae scrubbed while we hammered. Washing away dirt and grime. The lemony smell of dish soap carried through the air, reminding me of furniture polish and lightning.

I glanced at Tommy. He kept hitting nails as if his life depended on it, concentrating hard on each board in front of him. I had to admit, Tommy was a good worker.

Mae, on the other hand, left the porch half washed and went to do cartwheels in the yard.

When every nail was pounded tight and the rest of the washing was done, we stood back to examine our work. The boards lay flat with neat shiny nail heads reminding me of polka dots. Except for the holes, the porch looked great. But we looked a mess. Our faces were so dusty and grimy we might as well have been rubbing them with dirt.

There was something satisfying about swinging the hammer, hitting the nails, and fixing the porch. It made me feel strong. It made me feel powerful.

10 The creek

As we walked back to the Parkers', the sun beating down on us, cold water was all I could think about.

"Let's go to the creek," said Mae. "We can cool off and lie in the shade."

"Let's get some food first. I'm starving." I ran my arm across my forehead, wiping away the sweat. "Maybe Mrs. Parker will pack us some sandwiches."

"You want to come, Tommy?" When Mae asked that, I about fainted. I'd already spent half a day too much with Tommy Parker.

"I'm sure he doesn't want to tag along," I said. I gave Tommy a fierce stare, hoping he got the message.

"You girls won't be much fun," said Tommy.

I almost gagged. Like Tommy Parker was the mayor of Fun City.

"But since you asked me so nicely, Mae, I'll come anyway." Tommy gave me a grin. A snaky sort of grin, which meant he'd agreed for no other reason than to spite me.

Mae skipped along like she hadn't done anything at all. Sometimes she pays no attention to the things happening around her.

As we came through the kitchen door Mrs. Parker stared. She opened her mouth, but no words came out. I could tell she wanted to say something, yell at us for being so full of yuck in her spotless kitchen, but instead she shook her head, gave a long sigh, and shuffled us off to the bathrooms with wash-cloths and soap. I changed into frayed shorts and a T-shirt and gave Mae a clean shirt too, since hers was caked with front porch dust.

By the time we were all ready, Mrs. Parker had packed us ham salad sandwiches, all manner of things that crunched, and even glass bottles of Coke we had to promise to return so she could get her deposit back from the store.

Mama and I came to the creek together every summer. We'd picnic on a worn tablecloth, the checks faded from so much washing, munching on fried bologna sandwiches. Then she'd lie on the bank and soak up the sun while I searched for sala-manders and turtles.

Mae set out Mrs. Parker's food the second we got there. "Let's eat!" she said.

I plopped myself next to her and Tommy, then popped open my Coke. The first swallow tingled all the way down. Mae handed me a sandwich. I took a bite and grabbed a chip. The salt hit the spot after all that sweating. We didn't say much. The three of us simply sat there together, chewing and crunching, with the sun and the trees for company.

I lay back in the patchy grass. Even through my shirt I could feel where the rough green met bare dirt. I closed my eyes. Tiny white specks danced under my eyelids like fireflies.

"Delia," said Mae, "are you asleep?"

I turned my face toward her voice and squinted. "No, just lying here."

"Want to play in the water?"

"I do!" Tommy shouted.

The three of us waded in. After the stubby grass, the cool water felt soft. With arms outstretched, we moved like tight-rope performers at the circus, trying not to slip on the slick bottom.

I swear, there's nothing better than a cool creek on a hot summer day—the slippery rocks underfoot, the tiny minnows darting left and right. It was hard to pay attention to only one thing, with flashes of color everywhere.

A glimmer near my foot caught my eye. I reached down between two mossy rocks and pulled out a quarter.

"Twenty-five days of good luck for me!" I called to the others, holding it up in the sunshine.

I expected Mae and Tommy to hurry over for a look, but they didn't. They stared at the water as if there might be money everywhere—a pirate's treasure in Tucker's Creek.

"How do you figure that?" said Tommy.

"Well," I said, in my best teacher voice, "if you find a penny, that's good luck for the whole day. So a quarter must be good for twenty-five."

Tommy gave a *hmph*. If you asked me, he was being mean-spirited about my good fortune. Back to the old Tommy no one particularly liked. I smiled anyway. He wasn't going to ruin my day. After all, I was the one with the mama in the hospital. I needed more luck than anyone. I tucked the quarter in my pocket and then walked back to the bank and lay down on the grass.

With my eyes closed, I felt that quarter through the fabric of my shorts. Thinking about it brought to mind all those repairs at my house. Right then I whispered a promise to whoever might be listening up there. "I swear, if you give me seventeen days of good luck, I'll give the other eight away."

"Hey, Mae!" I shouted, rolling to my stomach.

Mae was standing in the creek studying a salamander as it crawled over her arm. She looked up.

"Think we could get jobs at Carmine's?" I called.

I could see Mae shrug. "I suppose," she called back. "Miss Carmine always has a Help Wanted sign hanging in the window."

I flipped back over and closed my eyes again, trying to remember all the shop windows in town. Mr. Pete at the hardware store had a sign up sometimes. Maybe there was an odd job that Miss Martha would be willing to pay for too. Mae had been right. Wood and nails and paint and patching—none of it was free.

"How do you get a job exactly?" I hollered to Tommy and Mae. It turned out I didn't have to yell—they were right there next to me, dripping water all over our picnic.

"Don't you go ask?" Tommy said.

Asking sounded easy enough. But maybe asking was like praying, which Mama always said didn't amount to a hill of beans.

Mae nodded. "I think Tommy's right. For babysitting the mom always calls you, but for a real job I think it's the other way around."

I sat up. "How do they decide if you're the right person?"

"I think they ask you questions to see if you have any special skills and how much you know about the job," said Mae. "A test, sort of."

Tests weren't my favorite. I got good grades, but even

the word *test* made me nervous. I lay back on the grass again, leaving Mae and Tommy to their lizard hunting or whatever they were doing.

Sunshine is helpful for thinking. It warms up the brain cells. With my brain warmed up and ready, I thought about my special skills—what I could say to someone to convince them to give me a job.

Good at math. (B last year.)

Excellent phone manners. (I'd taken calls at CJ's Diner, during Mama's shift.)

Neat handwriting. (A for penmanship.)

Willing to clean. (Not my favorite, but good at it when needed.)

Friendly to customers. (Unless their only customer was Tommy Parker.)

I wasn't sure what else might be important. Maybe that would be enough. I decided to make a few signs and post them around town. If Miss Martha let me tape one up at the post office I'd be all set. Everyone in town went to the post office.

11 Old Red's Flowers

I set my kickstand as quietly as I could in the gravel drive that runs parallel to Old Red's fence and leaned my backpack against the silver chain-link. Both of Rex's ears perked up. I could hear him sniffing for my scent. Rex couldn't see well anymore, but his nose worked fine.

The zipper on my backpack was almost silent as I tugged. Then I pulled out the scissors I'd taken from Mrs. Parker that morning. Mama's room needed flowers, ones that weren't in a frame. I wasn't stealing, really. More like borrowing, since flowers grow back.

There had always been something weird about Rex. All the other dogs in town loved kids. They'd come wagging with their heads cocked, as if they were asking for the time, and then they'd roll right over onto their backs once you started petting them. I'm almost certain that Rex, with his one jagged ear and missing patches of fur from fighting, never even dreamed about wagging.

Old Red's sunflowers were right next to where I'd parked my bike. There were green-faced ones with blazing yellow petals, some that started scarlet in the center and then faded to butter, and the kind with dark brown middles, same as in the picture in Mama's room.

Even when I was standing, the sunflowers were taller than me. I reached over the fence and took a thick green stalk in my hand. The bristles tickled. I didn't laugh. Rex was now at full attention. His low growl crept over the dirt and mulch.

I snipped one red-headed sunflower and set it gently on my pack. Then I reached for another. The screen door squeaked and Old Red walked out to the porch, bent over his cane. I crouched behind the fence, peeking through the leaves and thorns.

"What is it, boy?" he asked Rex, giving him a pat on his mangy head. Old Red sat on the white wooden swing that hung from the roof on tarnished metal chains, pushing off every now and then with his feet so he swayed a little. Rex lay back down, keeping one cloudy eye pointed in my direction.

I rose up like a cat, my spine unfolding inch by inch. My palms were sweating and it took me a few tries to cut through the thick stem of the next flower. I had planned to take just a few, but they were so pretty.

There was a rosebush no more than a foot away. It was covered in tight buds, with only one rose in full bloom. Creamy white, it reminded me of a wedding dress.

When I reached for the bush Rex lost his mind. He barked and snarled, his scarred face staring directly at me. Old Red stood, his eyes following Rex's gaze.

"Who's there?" he yelled. He picked up his cane and aimed it my way.

I shook the scissors, trying to get my fingers out of the handles, but they wrapped around me like a spider's web.

"Is that you, Delia Burns?" Old Red's voice was sharp as a blade.

I didn't answer. I was trying to grab my bike and zip my backpack and hold on to those flowers.

Rex ran down the porch steps. When Old Red saw where

Rex was fixing to go he must have taken a good look at his garden.

"Well, of all the no-good...," he mumbled. "You're stealing my flowers!"

I climbed on my bike, my feet feeling thick and clumsy. The blooms were clutched in my right hand, which was also trying to steady the handlebar.

When Rex hit that fence, his teeth bared and drool dripping from his cheeks, I about peed myself. The handlebar wobbled and I had no choice but to drop the flowers.

I looked back only once as I pedaled off. Old Red was standing there, shaking his cane. "Get out of here, you little thief!"

The clanging of Rex's collar hitting that fence rang in my ears.

I made it to the hospital in world-record time, my heart half out of my chest the entire way. Even after I'd set my bike in the rack and checked the road to be sure Old Red and Rex weren't coming after me, I was still panting, trying to catch my breath. Under my backpack I could feel my sweaty shirt sticking to my skin.

In a small patch of grass bounded by concrete, I noticed a clump of puny yellow dandelions. They came up in groups of three, leaning on one another, their stems thin and weak. I glanced around to see if anyone was watching, even though no one in their right mind would get angry at a girl picking good-for-nothing dandelions.

"Morning, Delia," said the security guard as I walked in, the sliding doors swooshing closed behind me. The guard knew everyone going in or out of that small hospital.

"Morning, Reggie," I answered, my words slow as molasses.

"Why the long face?" he asked.

I shrugged and stared at my pitiful bouquet.

There was an empty mug at the nurses' station near Mama's room on the third floor. I filled it with water, then dropped in the dandelions. Their fuzzy heads drooped.

I brushed Mama's hair and straightened the room, arranging the dandelions, plastic trays, remote control, and a few magazines that Mrs. Parker had brought in. While I worked I told Mama all about me and Mae and Tommy and the front porch. Then about that mean Old Red Clancy and how he and his dog had scared me half to death. He didn't need all those flowers anyway.

It was comforting to talk to her, even if she wasn't talking back.

It made me think of Miss Martha. She visited her husband's grave every week. We'd all seen her. Standing in the cemetery at the side of the Church of Christ, staring at the headstone, placing white carnations on the ground in a careful pattern, and talking up a storm. I used to think she was silly, talking to someone who couldn't talk back. I didn't think she was silly now.

Then, even though I wasn't convinced it would do any good, I decided to pray. I'm not sure why. I was getting used to it, I guess. The Parkers prayed at dinner, and I could hear Mr. Parker pray at bedtime too. He prayed aloud, not minding that all of us could hear him, his deep voice rising up and falling as it carried down the hall. He prayed for people he knew were sick or hurting and for me and Tommy too. He hadn't forgotten Mama yet, not even once.

I made sure the door to Mama's room was shut all the way. I didn't want anyone to hear me, in case my prayer wasn't very good. Then I closed my eyes tight.

"Hi, Lord, this is Delia. I'm Cassie Burns's daughter. If you make her better, I'll make sure she goes to church every Sunday and we'll be the first in line when the Salvation Army comes around. Uh, that's it, I guess. Amen."

I wasn't sure I could make deals like that with God, but I figured it couldn't hurt to try.

Mama liked to get a deal. She'd ask a salesperson flat-out, "Can I get this for ten percent off?" Even when there was no clearance sign. Sometimes they'd give it to her, sometimes not. It always made me want to run out of the store and hide.

"Delia," she'd say, "worst answer you can get is no."

12 church

Mrs. Parker's voice echoed through the house too early on Sunday morning. "Time to get cleaned up for church!"

I groaned and rolled over in bed, pulling up the patchwork quilt from where I'd kicked it during the night. The air in the room was already warm and the sun was shining bright through the lacy white curtains, but I kept my eyes shut and tried to pretend that it was still dark.

Noises from the kitchen floated up the stairs. I could hear bowls being pulled from cabinets and frying pans landing on the gas stove. Mr. Parker passed by my door, his steps heavy on the wood floor. The stairs creaked one by one. I imagined Mr. Parker nodding good morning to all his relatives, many of them looking like older, more agreeable versions of Tommy. As soon as he was downstairs the radio came on. Old-time southern gospel.

Sitting up in bed, I listened to the music of my new life. The deep bass of the quartet singer going on about the devil's long black train, the clinking of a spoon against a bowl as Mrs. Parker stirred pancake batter, the tick-tock of the grandfather clock in the living room that had once belonged to Great-Grandfather Parker, and, to top it all off, Tommy humming to himself as he got dressed across the hall. In all my life I never would have guessed he liked to hum.

I stepped out of bed and padded quietly to the door. The

lock made a faint click. I didn't want Tommy barging in while I was getting dressed. He'd seen enough of my underwear when I was moving in.

In the closet hung the three dresses I'd brought with me. A pink one trimmed with striped ribbon matched my new sandals best. I carefully took it off the hanger and pulled it over my knotted curls. My hair had a mind of its own, shooting whichever way it wanted no matter how much I brushed. I clipped a few strands away from my face with two super-sale barrettes and hoped for the best.

When I got to the kitchen, Mrs. Parker, a white apron keeping her Sunday dress safe from breakfast, was already stacking pancakes on a platter.

"Well now, don't you look sweet. Jack, doesn't Delia look lovely?"

Mr. Parker was tapping his fingers on the table, keeping time with the fast-picking banjo player on the radio. I remembered how his hands had felt that first night in the hospital, callused and strong. "She does indeed, dear. Lovely as a sunny day."

Then I heard a voice behind me. "What's so lovely?"

Leave it to Tommy Parker to ruin a good moment. I turned and stuck out my tongue. It wasn't very ladylike, especially not on a Sunday morning, but it felt good.

I sat down as Mrs. Parker poured orange juice and pulled bacon from the pan. It was Tommy's turn to say grace.

"Thank you, God, for the person who invented pancakes and syrup. Amen."

I grinned. That boy was stupid as all get-out, but I had to admit he was funny sometimes.

The parking lot of the First Congregational Church of

Christ was already bubbling over with cars and people when we arrived. It was the day of the church potluck dinner, and no matter where you looked, everyone, young and old, was carrying some type of dish. Large casseroles, small bowls covered with aluminum foil, and pans that could be only one thing: cake.

I had no idea so many folks went to church on a regular old Sunday. It was busier than CJ's Diner, and they served cheeseburgers and French fries—although with all the food walking through the door, the church might even have out-done CJ's.

Inside, the light was dimmer, filtering through multicolored stained glass, showing pictures of stories from the Bible. Mrs. Parker dropped off her corn bread for the lunchtime meal and then we took our seats. The pews were mostly full already, but the usher found us a spot near the front. You'd have thought that no one saw each other the rest of the week by the amount of chatter in that church. The only times I'd been to church Mama had shushed me the whole time.

I spied Old Red Clancy, wearing a drab brown jacket and pants. He was sitting alone in the back, reading a hymnal or maybe the Bible. I turned quick and slouched in the pew.

When the organ music began and the preacher took his seat near the pulpit, the room quieted. I flipped through the bulletin, reading about all the activities happening in the coming week. Tommy sat next to me, fidgeting.

I tried my best to focus on the service, standing up and sitting down when I was supposed to, reading the numbers listed on wooden signs in the front corners of the sanctuary and then finding them in the worn hymnal. The congregation enjoyed singing—that much was clear. There was clapping and swaying and a few men in the choir who sang deep and low like the songs I'd heard that morning on the radio.

When the preacher started preaching I was ready to sit down for a while. He paced across the front of the church, talking about miracles and loaves and fishes. As he spoke, an occasional cry of *Amen, brother!* or *Hallelujah!* or *Praise the Lord!* rose up from the congregation. Each time a voice called out, that preacher's energy grew. His words became louder and more forceful and he looked straight at me, like he could see directly into my soul, at all the good and bad sitting there.

I lowered my eyes and glanced at Tommy. He'd stopped fidgeting and was staring at the preacher fierce, barely blinking, like he expected something unusual to happen and didn't want to miss it. My stomach was starting to grumble. It had been hours since breakfast.

Glancing around the church, I could tell I wasn't the only one wishing the preacher would stop talking. Old folks were fanning themselves with their programs; little ones had given up, lying flat on the pews, their heads on their mama's lap.

Suddenly the preacher's voice cut through my thoughts. "Brothers and sisters, I think I could preach all day."

My eyes opened wide and Tommy and I turned to each other, our mouths hanging open. "I hope not," I whispered.

"Me too," he whispered back.

"But if I did that," continued the preacher, "we'd never get to dinner."

Tommy gave me a thumbs-up.

"The ladies have been cooking all week. Beans and corn bread, cherry pies and broccoli casserole. Sister Martha, have you blessed us with your fried chicken today?"

Everyone turned toward the back. Sure enough, there was Miss Martha, a wide grin on her face. "You know I did, Preacher," she answered.

God bless Miss Martha, because after another song and a prayer that felt as long as the sermon, the preacher finally let us go. Tommy and I ran outside, slipping past the handshaking and joining all the other kids whose legs were itching to run. A game of tag had already begun on the side yard, away from all the grownups, who were milling around front, catching up on the gossip they didn't get to share before the service.

After the last pew emptied, the preacher stood on the front steps, his arms raised high, his black robe hanging down like dark wings.

"It's time for dinner, now let's go eat!"

I followed the other kids charging to the church basement. Long tables were set up with vinyl tablecloths and plastic flowers popping up from chipped glass vases. We loaded paper plates with fried chicken, macaroni and cheese, green beans with thick bacon, and Mrs. Parker's corn bread. There were separate plates for dessert, which was a good thing, because in the back, taking up two whole tables against the wall, were fruit crisps and pies, wobbly Jell-O salads dotted with fruit, and all kinds of chocolate, brownies and cookies and cakes.

For a while as we talked and laughed and ate, I forgot about Mama being in the hospital. I forgot about feeling alone. Miss Martha sat down next to me a while later and started eating, dipping white bread into her baked beans.

"Miss Martha," I said, my mouth full, "this is the best chicken I've ever tasted."

"It's my mama's secret recipe, bless her soul," she whispered, leaning over. "I make it for every church dinner. Folks have gotten used to it, I guess."

"Don't you ever want to make something else?" I took a long drink of sweet tea.

"Well, child. Now everyone has a special gift. Some folks can sing while others are good with numbers. Me, I didn't get much in the way of gifts, excepting for that fried chicken."

Miss Martha kept talking, telling me how she once fried up chicken for more than two hundred people. I nodded now and then but didn't say a word. My mind was busy figuring. Figuring out if Miss Martha was right or if God had forgotten to give me a gift.

13 Baptism

Mae came over straightaway Monday morning, riding her bike as if the devil—or Rex, for that matter—was chasing her down the road. I was waiting on the front porch swing when I first saw her, the smell of Mrs. Parker's eggs and home fries still coming from the kitchen.

Mae had a backpack slung over both shoulders. By the time she pulled up to the house I was already standing in the driveway.

"What's in the bag?"

Mae's bike didn't have a kickstand, so she climbed off and laid it on the ground. "Some more things I thought might be useful from Daddy's tools."

She pulled the backpack off and unzipped the top so I could see in. "A wrench, a screwdriver, and this long thing with bubbles."

She held up what looked like two rulers with three tiny glass tubes glued in between. Each of the tubes was filled with water and a bubble of air. "I have no idea what it is, but I figured we might need it anyway."

Every time she shifted the rulers, the air bubbles in the tubes moved up or down, right or left. It was fun to watch, but seemed more like a toy than anything that might be useful in fixing a house.

"Oh, good, you brought a level."

When I heard Tommy Parker's voice my heart did a back flip. I hadn't heard him coming. He was good at sneaking.

"What's it do?" asked Mae.

I was glad she asked and not me.

Tommy took the level from her hand and set it on the driveway. All the bubbles moved to the middle of the tubes.

"Air in the center means whatever you're working on is flat. That it isn't tilted. Walls or floors that tilt are big trouble in houses."

I rolled my eyes in Mae's direction. "Duh. Everyone knows that."

When we got to my house Mae unloaded her supplies on the kitchen table. I wasn't hopeful that the measly assortment could handle all the fixing that was needed. Mr. Parker had a whole workshop in his garage. There were screwdrivers of all sizes lined up like dolls in a display, shiny steel wrenches, saws with one handle and two, their sharp teeth reminding me of sharks I'd seen on TV. I knew he fussed over each one, making sure it was clean and in the right spot. I wasn't about to ask him for anything.

"How many days left?" asked Mae.

"Fourteen," I said.

Tommy studied the list hanging on the refrigerator as if he might be tested on it when we went back to school after summer vacation. "I say we try fixing the leaky kitchen pipe."

Mae and I gave each other one of those looks meant for stupid suggestions.

Tommy must have seen it. "No, really. I've watched my dad do it. Usually leaky pipes only need tightening."

"Okay," I answered. I wasn't certain how to fix any of the other things anyway.

Tommy smiled. I couldn't help but smile back.

The three of us crouched near the open cabinet under the sink. Under the pipe was a dinner plate with a dishtowel on top. Mama put it there to catch the drips. She changed the towel each morning so it never got too wet. I picked up the plate with the soggy towel so none of us would accidentally break it.

Tommy had a wide wrench in his hand. He stuck his head inside the cabinet and tapped on the copper pipes. "Right here is the problem."

He pointed to where water was leaking out, one drop after another. The dripping reminded me of a line of ants, endlessly moving in the same direction. I wanted to say something about how it didn't take a genius to figure that out, but I didn't.

"It should be easy. Once I tighten it it'll be good as new." Tommy's words were firm and steady, which was surprising. It made him seem older and smarter and not quite so annoying. Part of me, a very small part, was a little bit glad Tommy was helping. He did know a fair amount about fixing.

I stood by the faucet twisting a curl of my hair. Mae started singing a new song from the radio. Unlike me, Mae had a beautiful voice. One of her gifts, as Miss Martha would say. My voice usually cracked like a duck with strep throat.

Tommy mumbled under the cabinet. Something about left or right.

"Do you know what you're doing down there?" asked Mae.

"Mm-hm," Tommy said.

First there was a popping sound. Then there was nothing but wet. Emergency-sprinkler wet. Water-spraying-in-every-direction-from-under-the-sink wet. In seconds we looked like we'd been in a swimming pool with all of our clothes on.

Mae and I screamed to high heaven. Now, you might think that we'd go running all frantic-like around that kitchen, or left the house entirely, but we didn't. We stood there with our hands half covering our faces as the water drenched us. Stood there like our feet were stuck in swamp muck and we had no place to go.

Tommy got the worst of it. That water could really have put an eye out. He stayed under the sink, though, cranking his wrench back and forth. I'd never seen his arm move so fast.

Then the water stopped. Mae and I kept standing there like department-store mannequins. Waiting for someone to give us a nudge and tell us what to do, I guess.

Tommy came out from under the sink and stood next to Mae and me. "The leak is fixed."

There was quiet and then there was only laughter. There we were, dripping wet as if we'd been baptized by the kitchen sink, laughing so hard we were gasping for air.

When we finally came to our senses I looked around. The entire kitchen floor was covered in water. There wasn't a spot the size of a mite that hadn't been hit.

"Lordy, lordy," said Mae.

"You sound like one of the gray-haired ladies down at the post office," I teased.

We all laughed again, which made the giant mess feel more silly than terrible.

I emptied the entire drawer of dishtowels and began tossing them to Mae and Tommy. We dropped to the linoleum and began mopping up that water, one square at a time.

With towels under our hands and towels under our knees, we moved slowly around the room, shining up that faded, dull floor.

When we finished, maybe it was only my imagination, but the kitchen seemed to sparkle. I went to the list, which had somehow remained dry, and with one swipe of my black marker, I crossed off the leaky pipe.

14 Help Wanted

That afternoon Mae and I sat on the front porch, paper and markers spread all around, figuring out what to write on my signs.

"They need to be colorful," said Mae. "Get people's attention. When Mom advertises, she always has big, bright letters."

Mae's mom sold Avon to almost every lady in town. Mama said she was "born for sales," which in Mama's book was not a compliment. Mae's mom was small, not much taller than me, but when she came into a room, everyone knew it. Maybe it was her clothes, which were so bright it was almost hard to look directly at her without sunglasses. Or maybe it was her flouncy blond hair that smelled of hairspray, or it could have been her eyeliner. Mae's mom didn't go anywhere without thick black eyeliner.

"Why don't you work on one and I'll work on another," I said. "Then we can compare."

Mae nodded.

I thought back to the creek and the talents I'd come up with dozing in the sun. At the top of the paper I wrote *Odd Jobs Needed* in bright blue. Then I listed my skills, each one in different color, pointing up and down and diagonal. When I finished, it was as if all the best parts of me were exploding in different directions.

"Think we should say anything about payment?" Mae asked.

"I didn't." I tried to see what she was drawing, but she had her arm around her paper, covering her work as if she was taking a test and didn't want anyone to copy her answers.

"What do you think?" I held my sign up for her.

"Great!" Mae held hers up too. It said, *Hard day? Call Delia and Mae.* Then it showed her phone number and cartoon drawings of us. Me with my crazy brown curls and wide eyes and Mae with her cute freckles.

We made a few more signs, then walked to town. Mae sang and skipped as usual. Sometimes being with Mae was like traveling with a soap bubble, the kind little kids made by blowing through those plastic sticks with circles on the ends. Mae sparkled and glimmered and floated along, going whatever direction the wind blew.

The post office was our first stop. Miss Martha greeted us as if we were long-lost friends. "Aren't you two a sight for sore eyes." She hugged us tight and offered us candy from a jar. "Unless you'd like a gum instead? I have gum in my pocketbook."

We shook our heads and unwrapped the candy.

"Miss Martha, Mae and I are looking for odd jobs to make some spending money. Would you mind me posting a sign here on your corkboard?" I asked.

There were all manner of postings on the board. One was for a lost dog named French Fry. French Fry was well known in Tucker's Ferry. He ran away at least once a month. Always made it home by himself, but his owners still hung up the signs. There was a car for sale and one paper that had tiny slips at the bottom cut like fringe with the name and number of someone who was interested in giving guitar lessons.

"Of course you can," Miss Martha said. "Here, let me clear some space." Down came the car for sale, crumpled up and tossed in the trash. "Everyone knows that car isn't even good enough for the junkyard," she said. "That Spurlock boy might as well admit it."

Signs were moved and organized until there was space for ours. Miss Martha stuck two silver tacks through the top corners. "You know, I could use some extra hands this week."

My ears perked up. Mae was busy fiddling with the locks on the post office boxes, turning them all so they pointed in the same direction.

"Come over to my house Wednesday morning, and wear clothes you don't care much about. I've got two bushel of cucumbers desperately wanting to be pickles. If we can get them all cooked and into Mason jars, I'll give you two dollars each."

"We'll be there, Miss Martha," I said. We had our first job already! "If you hear of anyone else needing help, be sure to point them to our sign."

At Carmine's Canine Salon it was like walking into a sauna, except for all the dog hair. Sure enough, Mae was right, Miss Carmine had a Help Wanted sign in the window. We told her we were looking for work.

"Stop by any day around four o'clock," she said. "If you sweep up, wash towels, and get the place back in order, it's worth ten dollars."

Mae was rubbing noses with a spaniel, so it was a good thing I was paying attention. "You've got it, Miss Carmine."

When we left the salon I started singing right along with Mae. There we were, two girl bubbles, floating down the street without a care in the world. A man with a carved wooden cane held the door for us when we got to Pete's Hardware. I felt like royalty as we walked inside, the jingly bells ringing to announce our arrival.

Mr. Pete wasn't there, but we found a spot on the front of the counter, near the one for the Friday-night fish fry at the VFW. I didn't hold out much hope for finding work at the hardware store. After all, people who bought things at hardware stores were usually handy. But it was worth a try.

Mae grabbed my arm as we walked out. We hooked elbows and swung in a circle, square-dance style. As luck would have it, I swung straight into Tommy Parker. He was a sharp pin, popping my good mood.

"Watch where you're going," he grumped.

"You watch where *you're* going, Tommy Parker."

We stared at each other. I narrowed my eyes, willing myself not to be the first to blink. I wasn't going to blink if my eyes dried up and started shriveling in my head. Not even if I died. They'd lay me out in the casket and there I'd be, my eyes still wide open.

Tommy blinked first. "I came to find you so we could get some ice cream. Mom gave me money for all of us."

Well, you could have knocked me over with a raisin when he said that. Tommy wasn't my favorite, but I wasn't going to turn down free ice cream, so down the street we went to the drugstore. It had an old-fashioned ice-cream counter in the back. There were five red stools with silver trim where you could sit and watch the soda jerks make the shakes and sundaes. All the stools were open. We sat down and swiveled back and forth a few times.

Mae ordered a butterscotch sundae. Then Tommy ordered and my mouth fell open.

"That's what I was going to get," I said.

As it turned out, Tommy and I both love strawberry ice cream with chocolate sauce and whipped cream. It's harder to hate someone when they like the same ice cream as you.

15 Pickles

Miss Martha's kitchen was littered with bubbling pots of cucumbers, clear Mason jars, rubber-lined lids, and golden rings to lock in all the juice. She picked a pot off the stove, her hands in faded green oven mitts. We watched her carry it to the table.

"Girls!" she yelled. "I need you to set something here so I don't burn my table."

I grabbed a dishtowel from the counter and laid it out for Miss Martha. She put the pot down and pulled off the lid. Steam poured out, adding to the already hot and wet feel of the kitchen. The air smelled so strongly of vinegar that my eyes watered.

"Well, I swan!" she said. "Those pots get heavier every year. One of these days they're going to break my back."

Mae and I were in charge of moving cooked pickles to the jars, then using a ladle to add juice until it almost reached the top. Mae put in the pickles. I added the juice. Miss Martha topped each jar with a rubber-lined lid. The heat from the pickles pulled the red rubber tight, sealing it fresh. One by one the clear jars turned green and were lined up on the long wooden table.

"Do you-all believe in angels?" I asked when I was waiting for more pickles to be ready.

"I do," said Mae. "But I've never seen one. I bet they're pretty, though, with shiny gold halos and white wings, exactly like the pictures in books."

I thought about an angel like that sitting on Mama's bed, stroking her hair and telling her stories about heaven. Maybe that was why she was still asleep. She really liked listening to those angels.

Miss Martha turned from the stove and wiped her hands on her faded blue apron. "Angels, you say? Well now, let me tell you a story."

We all sat at the table, the kitchen air a thick cloud of vinegar, sugar, cloves, and dill. Then Miss Martha started to talk.

"I was driving home once. Oh, it was years and years ago, back when my hair color didn't come from a box and all these wrinkles hadn't yet arrived. It was a terrible night. The rain was pouring in thick sheets. Even with the wipers going full speed I could barely see where I was going."

I took a fresh dill pickle slice from the bowl on the table and munched.

"There I was, my face almost pressed up against the windshield, when I noticed a hitchhiker on the side of the road."

"What was he doing out in the storm?" asked Mae.

"Lord only knows, child."

I kept munching pickles like they were popcorn at the movies.

"Well, I couldn't simply pretend I hadn't seen him there, looking like a drowned rat, so I pulled over." Miss Martha tilted her head to one side and tapped a finger on her cheek. "Can't remember a thing we talked about, but no matter." She looked at me and Mae. "Now, where was I?"

"He'd just gotten in the car," said Mae.

"That's right." She straightened her apron. "I drove him maybe five miles down the road. He thanked me kindly and climbed out. Then it was the strangest thing. Now mind you, the sky was still letting out. I cleared the foggy front window, rubbing it with my fist so I could see where he was going. But you know what?"

"What?" we answered in unison.

"I couldn't see heads or tails of him again. It was as if he'd vanished into thin air."

Half-chewed pickle went down my throat in a big gulp as I imagined what it would be like if Mae or Miss Martha went *poof*. If they were here, then gone, faster than I could blink.

Miss Martha's eyes darted between me and Mae; then she broke out laughing. "You should see yourselves. Eyes as big as doughnuts." She leaned against the kitchen counter.

"Do you think he was an angel?" I asked.

"Maybe he was, maybe he wasn't. I was glad I'd gotten him out of the rain for a few minutes either way."

"Let's say he was an angel," said Mae. "That means angels might be here right now, looking like normal folks." She glanced around the kitchen as if maybe there was one hiding behind all the Mason jars.

"It would be nice if they came for a visit every now and then." I was thinking about Mama.

Mae and I couldn't agree on anyone in town who might be an angel. She thought maybe Miss Jackson, the Bible school teacher, but I disagreed. I'd heard her cuss once at the grocery store when she dropped a jar and spaghetti sauce splattered all over the front of her dress. I'm no expert, but I'm fairly certain angels aren't allowed to swear.

Miss Martha kept on with the stories all afternoon. "I used to know these brothers. Last name was Hobson. Ornery lot, those Hobsons." Miss Martha's face pinched up like she still wanted to give one of them a swat. "Anyway, all the Hobsons, from the beginning of time, had these big ears. You could spot a Hobson from a mile away. Heck, even folks six counties over could spot them. Those boys couldn't run away if they tried. Everyone knew what house to bring them home to."

As the jars cooled, Mae and I screwed gold rings on top. We carried them two by two to Miss Martha's pantry, a windowless room next to her kitchen. The jars fit four deep on the bottom shelf. If I ever got a craving for pickles I knew where to come.

When Miss Martha pulled the next pot from the stove, we worked side by side.

"I heard you made a visit to Old Red the other day," she said, her voice quiet.

That made me stop ladling. In an instant, my insides felt tight. I looked at Miss Martha, but her eyes were focused on the pickles.

"You know, all those flowers in his yard belonged to his wife, Rosalea. She died a year before you were born." Miss Martha put her hands at the base of her back and stretched. "Rosalea sure did have a green thumb. I bet she could have planted a plastic seed in the fall and come spring it would have bloomed."

I pushed the ladle down into the murky green liquid. Bits of dill floated on the surface.

"Never met a nicer woman," said Miss Martha. "And that's God's honest truth. Old Red was like Mae here, always jumping from one thing to another. Rosalea was different, though. Rosalea had the patience of a saint."

"He's such a grumpy old man," I said.

"And his dog is meaner than a snake," said Mae.

Miss Martha shook her head. "Wasn't always that way. After Rosalea passed, Old Red reminded me of a wilted dandelion."

"Now he's all alone," said Mae.

We finished cleaning up the kitchen, Mae and me scrubbing pots, wiping down the counters and the table with wet dishcloths. All I could think of was Old Red with his chain-link fence and hateful dog, protecting Rosalea's flowers.

I walked Mae home, both of us smelling like a pickle factory. When we got there, Mae reached into her pocket and pulled out the two dollars Miss Martha had given her.

"Here you go, Delia."

"What are you giving me that for? You earned it fair and square."

"I want you to have it." Mae grinned.

"Really?" I asked.

Mae nodded.

"Thanks," I said, giving her a hug.

Mae's mom was in the living room, sorting tiny lipstick samples into piles. "Hello, ladies!" she yelled. It was easy to understand why Mae wasn't a good whisperer.

As we came closer, Mae's mom fanned the air in front of her nose. "Whooee! Stop right there. You girls need a bath." Then her eyes gleamed with an idea. "Or some perfume!" She held up a bottle like she was one of those models in a TV commercial.

Suddenly, without warning, small drops of perfume

were showering over us. We closed our eyes and covered our mouths, trying to breathe through the terrible fumes.

"Mom, stop!" Mae choked out.

When the air cleared, we smelled even worse. Pickles and perfume. I ran to the door, fearful that Mae's mom might get other beauty ideas.

"If you decide you want any perfume, Delia, you let me know!" she called after me.

16 Dandelions

Mr. and Mrs. Parker took Tommy and me to CJ's Diner for dinner that night. It felt weird to be there. When I walked through the front door, I half expected to see Mama standing behind the counter. All the other waitresses made a big fuss when I came in. They kept offering me milkshakes and double-dip cones and hot fudge sundaes, like ice cream might somehow bring my mama back.

After dinner we drove to the hospital.

There was a bulletin board outside Mama's room, and I read the announcements hanging there. The cafeteria menu was tacked up, with a special mention of homemade strawberry shortcake all week. A gold star cut from shiny paper was posted at the very top with a picture of a woman directly underneath. *Nurse of the Month*, it said. There was also a paper with big, bold print: *Killing Germs Saves Lives*. After I read about the importance of proper handwashing, I went to the nurses' station.

The nurses had a different kind of board posted on the wall next to where they sat. It listed all the patients they were responsible for. Room 316 was Mama. I picked up a piece of chalk and drew a heart next to her name, then joined the Parkers, who'd already made themselves comfortable, pulling in extra chairs so we all had a place to sit.

With the four of us telling Mama what was going on in

Tucker's Ferry, it was like being at the post office on Saturday morning. All we needed was Miss Martha. Mrs. Parker had brought the *Tucker's Ferry Dispatch* and read the local news, starting with the obituaries, which seemed to me a bad thing to be reading to someone lying in a hospital bed. I don't understand why grownups are so interested in reading about people dying.

"Oh my, Mrs. Bennett passed on Sunday. What a sweet lady. Says here she was eighty-seven. I remember when her husband died." Mrs. Parker glanced up from the paper. "Jack, when was that? Maybe five or six years ago now."

Mr. Parker thought for a moment. "Has it been that long?"

Tommy flipped through channels with the remote.

I was busy tending to Mama's nails while Mrs. Parker talked. Mama kept her nails short so she wouldn't bite them. They were always painted. I didn't want Mama to wake up with ugly nails.

With all the chatter, the TV blaring, and me rounding the edges of Mama's nails with a file, I could almost pretend that we were in the Glamour Nails Salon, which was next to Carmine's. Sometimes Mae and I looked in through the windows when we went by, imagining that we were Glamour Girls and wondering when our mamas would let us make an appointment to get glamorous.

As I brushed on a coat of Positively Pink, Mrs. Parker started in on the local business news.

"Pete's Hardware is having a sale this week on paint. Jack, do we have anything in the house that needs painting?"

Mr. Parker mumbled something from the corner where he was reading a sports magazine.

"Carmine's is offering a Thursday deal on grooming, two

for the price of one. I wonder if you get half off for one dog?" Mrs. Parker chuckled.

The second coat of Mama's nail polish was almost finished when Mrs. Parker turned to the weather page. Tommy and his dad left to go get us all a soda pop.

"Supposed to be beautiful all week, Delia. What great weather we've had this summer."

"All except for that storm," I said.

Mrs. Parker caught her lip between her teeth and touched my hand. I could tell she was wishing she'd said something else.

Her words didn't make me think about Mama, though; they made me think about my house and all the outside chores that still needed to be done. The roof especially.

"Penny for your thoughts, Delia."

"Oh," I said, sighing. "No matter how many new things I learn, there are still so many more that I don't know how to do."

"What a strange thing to be thinking about." Mrs. Parker folded the newspaper and placed it on her lap. "You know, though, I feel the same way sometimes."

I turned the polish lid tight and set it on the side table by the bed. Mama's nails were done. The good thing about her not moving was that the polish would dry without any nicks.

"What do you still have to learn?" I asked. "You're good at everything."

Mrs. Parker leaned over. In a hushed voice she said, "Want to know something I've never told anyone?"

I turned away from the window and looked at her. Mrs. Parker had drawn her shoulders together and crossed her legs, as if she was trying to make herself as small as possible.

"I can't ride a bike."

My eyes narrowed. "What?"

"Yep. It's true. I'm thirty-eight years old and I don't know how to ride a bike."

Well, you could have knocked me over with a piece of gum when she said that. "It's so easy!" I told her. "I can teach you how to ride."

Mrs. Parker had a doubtful expression on her face, the same kind she got when Tommy promised to clean his room.

"Really!" I added. Then I cocked my head to the side. "How come you never asked Tommy to teach you? Or Mr. Parker?"

Mrs. Parker shrugged, the corners of her mouth pulling it down in a frown. "I'm not sure. Pride, I guess."

I nodded but didn't say any more.

Mrs. Parker popped the paper open again, flipped through the last pages, and then set it down on the table next to Mama. She stood and began wandering around the room. Straightening the sunflower picture, which had somehow gotten tilted. Dusting the TV with a white lace handkerchief from her pocket. Running her fingers gently over the wilted dandelions in the mug on the window ledge.

"Dandelions are a good flower for you to give your mama," she said.

"Not really," I muttered, remembering the blooms that I'd left scattered on the ground near Old Red's fence.

"They are," she insisted. "You know, each flower has some sort of meaning. I'm not sure who came up with them."

"Like what?" I asked.

"Well, yellow roses stand for friendship, sunflowers for happiness."

"What do dandelions mean?" I said.

"Love and faithfulness," said Mrs. Parker. She shook her head. "I can't remember any more of them."

Mrs. Parker and I sat quietly for a minute. "You know," she said suddenly, snapping her fingers as if a great idea had just popped into her head, "you should stop over at Mr. Clancy's, dear. I bet he knows the meaning of every flower on God's green earth. I'm sure he would cut you a big bouquet that you could bring in for your mama. He'd probably appreciate the company too."

I knew that Old Red giving me flowers after what I'd done was about as likely as Tommy Parker becoming president of the United States of America. The thought of going back there made me sick to my stomach.

17 Family Pictures

When I heard Mr. Parker leave for work the next day, the tires of his truck chewing up the pebbly road, I climbed out from under my covers. Mrs. Parker was clanging around in the kitchen, and I could smell the coffee brewing. I waited on the edge of the bed, picturing her as she drank a cup on the porch, probably lost in thought as she looked out at Old Red's cornfield.

I stared at my reflection in the dresser mirror. I remembered Miss Martha's story about those Hobson boys and their big ears. I thought about how Tommy could see exactly where his pointy chin came from every morning when he walked downstairs, and how Mae was probably born loud, just like her mama. Which parts of *me* were hand-me-downs? There had to be Burns family pictures somewhere.

After the screen door swung closed I snuck into the hallway. Tommy wasn't humming or complaining, so I knew he was still sleeping. I crept down the stairs, listening for Mrs. Parker, even though I was certain she was on her usual walk to the corner store for the morning paper. Warm blueberry muffins sat on a plate in the middle of the table. I grabbed one and poured some milk to wash it down. Then I wrote Mrs. Parker a note and left it propped by a creamy white pitcher with tiny flowers.

The key didn't fit at first and I fumbled with the lock, shaking the handle. Once inside, I leaned against the door, still breathing hard from running. Out of habit I reached for my Rainbow Jesus. The smooth ceramic felt familiar, almost like a pair of well-worn shoes.

"Now, where would Mama keep pictures?" I asked him, picking him up and carrying him with me like a puppy.

I started in the living room closet. There were ratty quilts, a box of winter scarves and mittens, and leftover wrapping-paper tubes that were bent on one end from getting shoved into the corner. The shelves hadn't been cleaned in forever, and in no time my hands and shorts were smeared with dark, dusty smudges.

With the windows and doors closed, the air in the house felt hot and stale. Sweat began beading on my forehead as I slid a kitchen chair from cabinet to cabinet and climbed up to check the top shelves. I was hoping for a small box, maybe a shoebox tied with a ribbon. The kind I'd seen in the movies. Rainbow Jesus watched from the kitchen table.

"Where are they?" I asked him. "Surely Mama kept something!" My voice was louder this time. It felt good to yell.

Upstairs, I set Rainbow Jesus in the hallway next to the closet. I started making neat piles of everything inside, sheets and pillowcases, towels and washcloths. My heart skipped when I saw a box about the right size at the top. Standing tiptoe on a stack of towels, I grabbed it, hoping. I held my breath as I pulled it down.

It was filled with half-used bars of soap.

I'm not certain, but I think that's when I started to cry. I didn't care about neat piles after that. By the time Mrs. Parker found me I was in Mama's room, ripping things from the closet and hurling them across the room.

"Stop this, Delia."

I ignored her, pulling drawers from the night table and dumping them onto Mama's bed. Old lipsticks, receipts, a half-read romance novel with a silk-topped marker, all added to the mountain of stuff.

Mrs. Parker came around the bed and grabbed me by the arm. "Stop it."

Her grip fell loose as I whirled around, eyeing the room like a trapped dog, searching for a way to get out. I leapt onto the bed and jumped off the opposite side. It was a foot race to the next room. There was more pulling and dumping and screaming. Then there was Mrs. Parker.

She wrapped herself tightly around me and pulled me to the floor. Struggling didn't get me anywhere. Her arms were firm.

I stretched toward the closet. "They've got to be here *somewhere!*"

Mrs. Parker rocked back and forth, never letting me go. "Shush now, baby, you're all right."

Through all my fussing and yelling, Mrs. Parker kept rocking. Rocking and rocking until the fight was gone. I felt like an empty paper bag as I buried my head in her chest and cried. She stroked my hair and my back and then hugged me stronger, her arms like a winter scarf trying to keep out the cold.

I don't know how long we sat there. But there came a point when my breathing was back to normal and the tears had stopped.

"I need a tissue," I said.

Mrs. Parker and I looked at each other. Her eyes judged

me, figuring out what I would do. Then she opened her arms and I was free.

In the bathroom I grabbed a wad of toilet paper to blow my nose. I stared at my reflection. Wild hair. Puffy red eyes. Dust and dirt and tears covering me like camouflage.

When I mustered up my courage and walked out, Mrs. Parker was waiting for me in the hall. She set a hand on my shoulder.

"What are you looking for exactly?"

"Pictures," I said.

Mrs. Parker stared at the hallway, which was still white from the fire extinguisher. I thought she was looking at the hole, but then she said, "Did you try up there?"

I followed her gaze. Sure enough, there was a door in the ceiling at the very end of the hall. I swear it was the first time I'd ever seen that door. It had appeared out of thin air, the way white-tailed bunny rabbits do at a magic show.

There was a thin cord with a metal bell-shaped pull. Mrs. Parker reached up, and as she pulled, the door creaked open and a set of stairs appeared, doubled up like a heavy backpack. The stairs unfolded all by themselves, as if they wanted me to climb.

I glanced at Mrs. Parker, and she nodded. "Go on. Maybe your mama put them in the attic."

The stairs shook, or maybe it was my legs. I crossed my fingers that the lightning and the rain and the fire hadn't destroyed whatever might be up there. Hot air blew down into my face. It smelled of wood and dust and pine trees.

"Do you see anything?" asked Mrs. Parker, her question bright and hopeful.

I stepped up and turned in a full circle, eyeballing every empty inch, including the plastic-covered hole in the roof. Mama didn't believe in praying, but it was all I had. With my eyes closed tight I prayed like I had cried, hard and fierce.

When I opened my eyes, I noticed a scrap of paper in the corner directly above Mama's room. As I walked, the broad wooden boards creaked. A short wall stood a few feet from the end of the house, creating a small hiding space that couldn't be seen from the stairs.

"There's a box!" I yelled down to Mrs. Parker. Curls stuck to my sweaty forehead and cheeks. I pushed them back and tucked them behind my ears.

The cardboard flaps were folded over one another. As I tugged them open, dust flew into the air and caught the light. I hoped it was the kind of dust that made children fly or wishes come true.

"Did you get it open yet? What's inside?" Mrs. Parker's voice sounded miles away.

I stared into the box. It wasn't filled with pictures. It wasn't filled with anything but outdated magazines and a majorette's baton.

Mama was right. Praying didn't get you anywhere.

18 Quilting Club

The quilting club of the First Congregational Church of Christ met every Friday at ten a.m. in the room next to the kitchen. They called themselves the Thread-Bears. Seeing the church program on Sunday had sparked an idea that had smoldered all week.

In the basement hall, my back against the cold, white-painted cinder blocks, I waited, clutching my garbage bag. Mae was supposed to come too, but besides having a whispering problem, Mae wasn't so great with being on time.

I figured it would be Granny Central. Boring, gray-haired ladies with knee-high pantyhose complaining about their arthritis and snacking on bite-sized prunes. I braced myself, ready to talk extra-loud so their hearing aids would pick up my voice.

The first thing I noticed was the music. Country music. The kind Mama listened to. The second thing was the table of cookies. Chocolate chip and sugar, which had that misshapen homemade look about them. The third thing to draw my attention was a familiar voice.

"Hi, Delia, I didn't know you liked to sew." It was Sarah, the fancy girl from my school.

I was so surprised that my words stuck in my throat for a minute. "I don't."

Her eyebrows crinkled.

"I mean, I don't yet, but I was hoping I could learn."

Sarah motioned and I followed her further inside. "Everyone, this is Delia. She needs some sewing lessons."

Hi and *Hello* came from around the room. Women lifted their eyes from their stitching, fingers tight on their needle. Some had hoops, the fabric tightly stretched in between the wooden rings. Others held directly to the fabric.

I set my bag down on the floor and grabbed an empty seat next to Sarah. She had a white sewing machine, not much bigger than a toaster, set up on a table. A pedal on the floor was attached by a thick black cord.

"You like to quilt?" I asked.

Sarah shook her head. "No. I make clothes. One day I'm going to be a fashion designer in New York City."

"That's right," said one of the ladies. "Sarah is going to be the very first world-famous designer from Tucker's Ferry, West Virginia. Yes indeed."

I smiled. I could hear snippets of conversation from every corner—"That New York is too big for me" and "Only the Lord will take me out of Tucker's Ferry."

"Do you make all your own clothes?" I remembered seeing her by Grey's Bakery, her outfit so department-store perfect.

"Not all of them. I don't make pants yet, or long-sleeved shirts, but I'm great with dresses. This is my newest one." She stood up quick and struck a pose.

I admired Sarah's dress, touching the detailed stitching at the hem, and then I glanced around the room. Each woman stared intently at her own project. All the women would raise the fabric closer to their eyes as they found the exact spot for the next stitch, then lower it as they pulled the colored thread through, raising their arm up high at the end to make sure it was tight. Sometimes they turned the fabric over, fussing and tugging to loosen a knot. Everywhere I looked, hands moved up and down. There was conversation now and then, but mostly it was quiet, except for the music.

Sarah nodded at my bag. "So what did you bring to work on?"

From the garbage bag I took out a window screen. The mesh was torn in several places, which was why the mosquitoes always made it in at night. My heart was pounding and my tongue felt swollen. I thought of Mrs. Parker not knowing how to ride a bike. Then I took a deep breath. "Think you can teach me how to sew this?"

My left hand clutched the garbage bag while my right held tight to the screen, ready to shove it back in when Sarah laughed. She didn't laugh, though. Instead she reached out and felt the material between her fingers.

"I was hoping it was a dress," she said. Her words sounded flat and disappointed. "Take a look in that bin over there. It's full of extras nobody wants."

"But what do I need?"

"Oh," said Sarah, already turning back to her sewing machine, "look for a clear thread. Like fishing line."

In the bin and assorted tin cans on a table near the wall I found supplies. I sat back down and took the screen in my lap, holding it the same way the other women held their fabric. Sarah was feeding pieces of what I imagined would be another new dress under a metal foot on her sewing machine. The needle bobbed in and out so fast I could barely see it.

I watched the others, licking the thread and pushing it through the eye of the needle. I knotted the thin line around a square of mesh and then copied the woman closest to me as I drew the needle up one side of the tear and down on the other.

I'd planned to stop at Old Red's after leaving the quilting club, but I went back to the Parkers' first. I made my bed, tucking the sheets in so tight I could have bounced a quarter off the edges. Then I ate lunch, even though I was still full of cookies and felt like I might throw up after every bite. I cleaned the kitchen with Mrs. Parker, ran the sweeper, plumped the pillows on the couch, and filled up every salt and pepper shaker she had.

Mrs. Parker must have gotten tired of me because she shooed me out of the house like I was a fly. "Go outside and play, honey. Find Tommy. He's around here somewhere."

I didn't look for Tommy. Instead I grabbed my bike and pedal by pedal I made my way to Old Red's. His house was only a few blocks away, but it felt like half a county over.

I leaned my bike against the chain-link fence and stood by the gate. The screen door was closed, but the door behind it was open.

"Mr. Clancy," I called. My voice caught in my throat. I watched for movement in the windows. There was nothing, not even a growl from Rex.

"Hello!" I yelled. "Mr. Clancy!"

Rex came to the door, his head low, his half-blind eyes on me like I was his last supper.

"What is it, boy?" Old Red stared at me through the screen, leaning heavily on his cane. Then he pushed the door open and came onto the porch, Rex at his heels.

"Afternoon, Delia Burns," he said. His voice reminded me of coarse sandpaper.

With hands clasped behind my back, I stared at the loose rock under my feet. A beetle lay on his back near my toe, his legs flapping this way and that, trying to right himself. The air was hot and still.

"Afternoon, Mr. Clancy," I said. I forced my gaze up until I could see his shoes. Worn leather house slippers, with sock-covered toes poking out the front. "Can I come in?"

He held his cane in front of Rex. "Stay." Then he nodded in my direction.

I lifted the horseshoe lock and pushed the gate. It creaked like it hadn't been opened in a hundred years. When it was locked again, I turned and stepped into Rosalea's garden.

Flowering, creeping vines with thick stems crisscrossed a black iron arch. Green leaves with blooms as white as pearls hung like spider webs. I pushed them away from my face. Inside the garden, the rough rock was replaced by smooth stepping-stones. Between them grew a blanket of thick jade moss.

I tiptoed from stone to stone. "You can walk on the moss," said Old Red. "Won't hurt it none."

I took another step and stopped. Even though I didn't mean to, I breathed deep, letting that perfumed air reach all the way down to the bottom of my toes.

"Assume you came visiting for a reason," said Old Red. He tapped his cane on the step, like he was counting seconds until it was time for me to leave.

"Yes sir," I said, swallowing hard. "I wanted to apologize for cutting your flowers."

"Go on, then."

I watched a toad hop across the path, then disappear into the foliage. Lucky toad, I thought.

"I'm sorry I cut your flowers, Mr. Clancy."

"*Stole* is more like it." He crossed his arms in front of him, the cane dangling near his wrist. Rex growled.

"My mama is in the hospital. I wanted to bring her something pretty."

"Didn't have to steal," he said, his voice cold as a shadow. He stared out into the road as if he was watching for someone else. As if I wasn't standing right in front of him.

With tight fists at my side, I marched directly up the steps, until I was only a foot away from him and Rex. "*I know*. Which is why I'm here. I didn't mean to take Rosalea's flowers."

When I mentioned Rosalea I saw the surprise in his face, as if hers was the last name he expected me to mention. His mouth softened for a moment, and I thought maybe he was going to apologize then for being so mean. Invite me in and offer me a glass of lemonade.

He didn't.

The softness I'd seen hardened like clay and his wrinkled face seemed to shrink right in front of my eyes. "Don't you *ever* cut my flowers again. Or I'll call the police." He said *police* like it was two long words.

"Fine," I said. I stomped down the steps and toward the gate, squishing that spongy moss beneath my sneakers with every step. "I wouldn't want any of your flowers even if you gave them to me. Even if you *begged* me to cut them. Even if they were the very last flowers on earth!"

Stupid Miss Martha and Mrs. Parker, I thought as I pedaled home. This was all their fault.

19 curtains

The gardening book I'd checked out from the library had a warning about ivy. *Ivy kills.*

Unfortunately for me, there was ivy growing all over the brick walls of my house. I wasn't sure how a little plant could kill a brick, but I figured if it was printed in a book it had to be true, so I pulled and pulled.

One hour later, sweat dripping down my skin under the long-sleeved T-shirt and jeans Mrs. Parker had made me wear, my fingers stiff and muscles cramping from fighting that nasty green, I was ready to die.

Ivy is a lot stronger than it looks.

Bits of mortar flew out from between the bricks as I yanked, landing by my feet in the grass. Sometimes the brick came loose completely. I glared at the evil roots growing out the side of the vines, which had weaseled their way even into hard-as-rock places, and I stacked the loose bricks in a pile. I'd have to get to those later.

After a while I was ivy'd out. I stood in the front yard and stared at the flowerbeds. Brown-stemmed bushes with only a handful of leaves had somehow managed to live. There were half-dead tulips from spring that had never bloomed. They'd grown leaves but no flower. I wasn't sure how that was even possible. There were purple balls blooming at the tip of tall green stems, but I knew those were just wild chives. Weeds.

Suddenly Mrs. Parker came walking across the grass, a large silver thermos in her hand. "Water?" She held up a plastic cup. Then she poured me a cold drink. I'm telling you, I'd never tasted anything so sweet. It was almost better than Miss Martha's sun tea.

Mrs. Parker set the thermos on the porch step, then squared her shoulders. "Delia, I am ready for a bike lesson."

Anything that didn't involve yanking or digging or roots sounded good to me.

As we wheeled my bike to the flat stretch next to my house, I thought back to the night of the storm. I remembered running over the wet ground to the Parkers' in my bare feet, the long blades of grass grabbing, almost biting at my legs.

"My bike is too short for you, but that means it'll be easy to put your feet down to stop." I held the handlebars steady so Mrs. Parker could climb on.

She sighed. "I don't know why I'm so afraid of bikes. Makes no sense."

I waited for Mrs. Parker to get settled and then stood behind her. "I'm going to hold on to your shoulder." That was how Mama had taught me.

Mrs. Parker pushed one pedal down. She was squeezing the grips so tight that the color had drained from her hands. The bike moved an inch and she lurched forward, her feet heavy on the ground with panic.

"Don't give up," I said. "You're doing just fine."

She tried again and again, turning one pedal and then the other, losing her balance and finding it again. Together we made big loops around the yard, her wobbly steering becoming steadier with each turn. After we'd crossed the empty lots between the Parkers' house and mine a thousand times, I let go and ran alongside.

Mrs. Parker took off down the road, tottering a bit in the gravel, but she kept going. I watched her round the corner, then caught sight of her through the trees and the bushes as she pedaled along the block behind our street. I waved when she glanced my way.

When she finally pulled up in the driveway I cheered, "You did it!"

She smiled, her cheeks reminding me of pink bubblegum. "I did, didn't I? You're a good teacher, Delia."

I grinned as I sat down on the front steps. My face felt warm and I wondered if it was as bright as Mrs. Parker's.

"Any water left?" she asked.

When I shook the thermos I could tell it was empty.

"I'll get some more," I said. In the kitchen I automatically checked for dripping under the sink. It was dry as a desert under there. I'd always thought of Tommy in the same category as a sweat bee, annoying and useless, but he'd done a good job on the pipes.

Mrs. Parker followed me in while I poured us each a glass of tap water. She eyed the kitchen, then walked back to the living room, making small clicking noises.

"Know what this house needs, Delia?"

I knew what the house needed like I knew the difference between a hippo and a tadpole. But before I could recite any of the items on the list, Mrs. Parker said, "Curtains. Colorful curtains would give these rooms life. I'll go get my measuring tape. Consider it a thank-you."

She was back in minutes, her face still flushed from the

bike riding. "Look at these fabrics I found downtown last week. I didn't have a project in mind, but they were so lovely I had to buy them." She waved a few small scraps of brightly colored material in the air. I caught a glimpse of lime green, turquoise, and sunflower yellow.

"Oh, Mama would like this," I said, pulling out one of the pieces.

I watched as Mrs. Parker moved a chair to the front window and stood on it, one arm stretched out, trying to balance the measuring tape across the wide picture window. Every time she had it within a hair of the end, the tape would go limp as a noodle and fall to the floor.

"Here, I'll hold the other side," I said.

Together we measured. Mrs. Parker wrote down all sorts of notes and diagrams and numbers. Then she sat, tapping a pencil in one hand, while she drew different shapes of curtains.

"What do you think of this one?" She held up her paper.

I grimaced.

Her eraser went wild. Then she sketched again. "What about this one?"

I must have made a face without even knowing it because Mrs. Parker gave a long sigh and simply flipped the pencil to erase again. "But it's better than the first one," I said.

When she held up the third picture I smiled. "Perfect."

"Delia!" called a voice from outside.

It was Miss Martha. She stepped out of her white Chevette, which was old as sin, according to my mama, with a large envelope in one hand.

"Mercy me!" she said, staring at the heap of ivy. "You've been working hard."

I led Miss Martha into the house, where Mrs. Parker was holding her fabric samples up against the wall.

"And fixing up inside too! Delia, your mama is not going to believe her eyes."

The toe of my sneaker scuffed the wood floor.

When I finally looked up, Mrs. Parker's eyes were shining. Like the tears were all lined up, waiting for permission to fall. "She'll come home, baby, you wait and see."

"I'm going to get some more water," I said. In the kitchen I sat down at the table, rested my chin on my hands, and closed my eyes. There was still roofing and wiring, plumbing and flooring, patching and painting and other stuff I didn't have a name for. We'd fixed a few things and done some gardening and decorating, which made the house look way better. I tried to convince myself that every little bit mattered.

"I almost forgot what it was I came over for," said Miss Martha as she pulled out a chair. "This arrived for your mama today. It looked important, so I figured I'd best bring it right over."

The dark gold envelope was about the size of a sheet of paper, but thick as my thumb. I didn't recognize the return address. Someone had stamped the front with red ink. *Second Notification.* Mama and I didn't get much mail other than bills, so I wasn't too hopeful that this envelope was bringing good news like us winning the lottery or a timeshare at Myrtle Beach.

Mrs. Parker handed me a dull knife. I slid it under and across the flap to cut the seam. I reached in but stopped short, one hand holding the stack of papers, the other lifting the top of the envelope. The words in big, bold print on the top page were hard to miss. *Condemnation Notice.*

If Miss Martha and the Parkers knew about the inspector, then chances were good that there would be whispering and pointing next time I went to town. Mama never paid attention to Tucker's Ferry gossip. "Why would I care what someone else thinks about me?" she'd say. I wasn't as strong as Mama.

"Oh, this is nothing," I said in a louder voice than usual, leaning over the table. My hands lay on top of the packet of papers as if they might try to get up and leave.

Miss Martha and Mrs. Parker stared at me, their faces full of questions.

I said it one more time. "It's nothing."

20 carmine's canine salon

I almost forgot about Carmine's the following Wednesday. When I flew around the corner and skidded to a stop, Mae was waiting at the front door. Miracle of all miracles, she was on time for a change. I guess living right upstairs helped.

Inside the salon it was hot as a wool sock, and equally uncomfortable, with dog hair floating through the air like dandelion fluff.

"Oh, girls, you've got perfect timing," Miss Carmine said. "Grab some brooms and sweep all this up for me."

Mae and I started on different sides. As soon as I'd get a pile of fluff together, one of the blow dryers would start and all my hard work would fly away across the floor. Dog hair doesn't clump together like hairbrush hair. It likes to scatter. I got good at sensing when Miss Carmine was going to turn the switch.

There was a big trash bag of hair and nail clippings when we finished. Together Mae and I tied the top and carried it outside to the dumpster that sat out back in the alley.

"Mae, you're shedding." I couldn't help but laugh. We were covered in dog hair from head to toe.

Mae wiped her hand across my forehead. "There's white hair on your eyebrows. You look like my granny."

Anyone walking past would have thought we were nuttier than a pair of squirrels.

We came to our senses when Miss Carmine yelled from

the front, "I'm not paying you to giggle. Get back to work!"

She stopped us at the back room and pointed to a mountain of towels. "Either of you ever done laundry?"

I nodded, thinking back to mornings at the Speedi-King with Mama.

"Good. Here's the detergent." She pointed to a plastic tub, big enough to bathe a baby in, filled with white powder. "Half a scoop per load."

We started shoving towels in the washer. It was exactly like the washers at the Laundromat, except it didn't take coins. While the first load was running, we walked the salon, wiping down anything with hair on it and putting away the bottles and brushes that had been used during the day.

When load number one was in the dryer, spinning away, the back room became hotter than a rainforest in the middle of August. Sweat puddles formed by my feet. I'd seen pictures at the library of people standing in the jungle, naked as jaybirds. I always wondered why anyone would walk around without any clothes. Now I knew.

Mae was tossing in towels for another load of wash when she stopped, her face screwing up as if she had a mouthful of lemons.

"What?" I asked.

She grabbed a towel and brought it closer to her face. Then she pretended to puke. "You've got to smell this, Delia. Whatever is on these towels is the worst stink ever."

I took a whiff and doubled over. "Miss Carmine!" I yelled. "What in heaven's name is on these towels?"

She left a half-shaved, half-puffy poodle standing there on the grooming table while she came to check. Then she explained what the smell was. And where it came from. Mae eyed the towels as if they were radioactive.

We finished the wash as fast as we could after that. Mae held her nose and added towels to the washer one at a time, holding them as far out as possible and dropping them in the machine as if they might explode. I folded clean, warm towels and set them in neat stacks so Miss Carmine would be ready for the next day.

When we got our ten dollars, I was never so happy to be done with something in my whole life. It was even worse than ivy pulling. And that was saying something.

"Will you girls be back tomorrow?" Miss Carmine leaned against the front door frame, her arms folded across her chest.

Mae and I caught each other's eyes. "We might be busy tomorrow, Miss Carmine," I said. It wasn't really a lie—*might* was a word with possibility.

"That's what I thought. Have a good night, girls. Thanks for coming today."

As we left, Miss Carmine put her Help Wanted sign back in the front window.

"No more jobs," said Mae as we walked down the street. "They all stink."

I had to agree.

It's strange how someone can look so normal but be so lost. If anyone else had seen Mama, they'd have thought she was sleeping. I knew she was somewhere else. Not quite here on earth, but not quite in heaven either.

"Hey, Mama," I said after I kissed her cheek.

I went through my usual routine, plumping pillows,

wiping away imaginary dust on the windowsill, and arranging flowers. This time I had wildflowers—white Queen Anne's lace and pink phlox that I'd cut from the bank of the creek. They looked better than Old Red's fancy flowers anyway.

"The inspector sent another package."

Her hand was soft in mine, the warmth of her skin comforting. I touched her over and over again.

"We've got five more days," I said, almost as if I was telling myself. "Fixing takes longer than I thought it would."

I tried to keep my voice bright as a birthday. It was a good thing she couldn't see my face.

"There are flowers here, Mama. You should open your eyes and take a look."

I waited, as if my telling her to open her eyes would make it happen.

"When you get home to our fixed-up house, we should plant some flowers. It would be wonderful to have color blooming all summer long, don't you think?"

Mama didn't answer. I wondered if she'd ever answer me again. The last time she'd been herself, the night of the lightning, she'd been so angry. She didn't look angry anymore. I suspected that wherever she was, someone was making her feel a little better.

"I hope you have angels with you," I said. "Angels in sunflower-yellow T-shirts."

I wasn't sure, but I thought I saw Mama's hand move when I said that. I stared and stared, judging the distance between her fingers and from her painted nails to the stitches on the blanket. Every now and then her hand blurred and I had to blink to see clearly again. As soon as I reopened my eyes her fingers seemed closer together, the evenly spaced stitching nearer than it had been. I willed her hand to move again, but it didn't.

"What do the angels look like, Mama? Do any of them have curly hair like me? I bet they have beautiful voices."

I waited and Mama spoke.

Well, she mumbled. I held my ear close to her mouth and tried to make out the words, so excited I must have looked like Christmas morning. Mama was in there somewhere and she could hear me!

A nurse came running in when I pressed the call button. I was practically shouting what happened, grabbing Mama by the shoulder and shaking her to wake up. The nurse called in others. Soon enough the room was full of folks in white coats and hospital scrubs. With a long stethoscope they listened to her heart, then opened her eyelids to shine a bright light in her eyes.

Since it was when I mentioned angels that she spoke, I kept up that line of questioning. "Do they really have wings, Mama? Are they friendly? Have they been telling wonderful stories?"

I stood there for a long time, wishing and waiting for Mama to do something. Cough. Hiccup. Cry even. All those doctors and nurses and I listened closely, but no matter what we tried, we couldn't get her to say another word.

21 Measure Twice, Cut Once

I was running out of time, so Mae and me were back at the house the next morning. Seeing as our fixing skills were limited, we decided to tackle the windows. Those windows were so dirty it always seemed cloudy inside, even on a sunny day.

"Miss Martha said to use vinegar," I said, pulling a bottle from the cabinet. Mae held out a tattered rag and I poured some on.

Mae gagged. "More vinegar? It's like Carmine's, but worse!"

I nodded as I poured some on my rag too. Then I plugged my nose. "Let's get it over with." My voice sounded like I was talking through one of those fast-food restaurant intercoms.

We rubbed circles on that glass until our elbows about collapsed. Sure enough, that vinegar did the trick. We went from room to room, the house getting brighter after each stop. It reminded me of Miss Martha's. My entire house smelled like a jar of boiling pickles.

When we finished, Tommy was outside, even though I hadn't asked him to come. He was measuring the spots on the porch where the worn-out wood had given up. I stepped directly over him and down the steps to see what he had put in a pile in the yard. There were some pieces of scrap wood, a hammer and nails, and a jagged-edged saw.

I skimmed my fingers over the metal teeth.

Tommy handed Mae a tiny notepad and pencil. "You're in charge of writing everything down."

"What about me?" I asked, one hand on my hip.

"You're responsible for measuring." Tommy's voice sank deeper than usual, his chin almost touching his chest. "Measure twice, cut once." He grinned. "My granddad used to say that."

Mae pulled out the yellow metal tape and held it over the first hole. I got down on hands and knees to see the markings better. "Six and one-quarter inches," I said.

Mae quickly scribbled, then relayed the number to Tommy with a shout even though he was standing so close she could have balled up the paper and hit him with it.

"You sure?" he yelled back. "I don't want to cut it again."

I thought about giving him an eyeball, but he was fussing with the saw.

"Let's check." Mae pulled out the tape one more time.

I stared so hard the numbers might as well have stood up and smacked me in the face. A new piece of wood would need a tiny bit of space on each side to fit exactly right. "Six and one-eighth inches, Mae. And yes, I'm sure."

Mae crossed out the first number, jotted down the new one, as if she might forget it at the very second she needed to tell Tommy, and shouted again. After Tommy cut the wood, he gave it to her. She held it up to the light with a frown. "Is it supposed to look like that?"

Tommy scowled. It was the kind of scowl that told me plain as day he wasn't cutting another piece for that hole.

Mae held the good-enough piece in place while I pounded in the nails. The gaps in the wood had reminded me of missing teeth. Now they only looked a bit roughed up, like they'd been in a fight. No one was going to fall through, but they might stop and stare.

When the holes were patched, the three of us sat on the porch steps. Jagged leftovers of scrap wood sat heaped in the yard. The rinsed-out rags, still damp, hung over the porch railing, drying in the sun.

"Now what?" I said.

Tommy's great idea was to start working on the roof. "The longer that sits open, the worse it'll be," he said. As if he was the biggest roof expert in Tucker's Ferry.

The three of us walked out to the yard and stared at the top of the house.

"There is no way your daddy would let you up there," said Mae.

Tommy crossed his arms firmly in front of his chest. "Sure he would. I've been on a roof with my granddad. Besides, I'm not planning to fix it right yet, only take a good look and see how much needs to be done."

"I don't know, Tommy," I said. "Maybe Mae's right." I chewed the edge of my thumb as I tried to picture Tommy all the way up on top of the house.

With a *hmph*, Tommy turned toward home, leaving Mae and me standing there. After a minute we lay down in the cool grass, our hair spread out behind us, our fingers almost touching.

"Tommy's mad," said Mae as I watched a heart-shaped cloud float across the sky.

"He'll get over it. If Mrs. Parker found him on the roof she'd tan his hide. He wouldn't be able to sit for a month."

"Think he's coming back?"

"I doubt it."

We lay like that for a while. I thought about whales and

vinegar, lightning and roses, my new sandals and Miss Beatrice whacking the living daylights out of that cocoa machine. That inspector didn't come to mind even once.

A sharp metallic sound cut through my daydreaming. When I sat up, there was Tommy, dragging a long, silver ladder. It clanged as it bounced over the uneven ground. Judging by Mae's expression, she was as surprised as me to see him there. Tommy didn't say anything. His mouth was clamped tight. He leaned the ladder on the house, positioned it so the top stuck out over the edge of the roof, and began climbing.

"What do you think you're doing?" I asked.

Tommy ignored me, his face sour. Then he turned around as if he was going to say something after all. His weight shifted and that ladder began to sway in our direction.

"Tommy!" I yelled. Me and Mae grabbed the metal rungs and pushed with all our might, tilting it back toward the house.

It hit the edge of the roof with a thud. Bits of shingle fell to the ground.

I fixed my eyes on Tommy and shook my fist. "Now look what you've done!"

"Yeah," added Mae. "Delia doesn't need you to break anything else."

"Get down here this instant," I said, trying to sound like Mrs. Parker.

"I will not. You girls don't know anything. Roofing is man's work."

"You're a man?" I asked as Tommy climbed the last few steps to the top.

He walked across the roof to the lightning hole, his steps shaky. Getting his legs under him, he stood tall and gave us a glare as if to say he'd been fixing roofs his entire life. Then he crouched down near the edge of the plastic and started measuring. Thinking that maybe I should get up there myself and make him come down, I grabbed a rung and began climbing. A few steps up, that ladder was shaking worse than me. I was afraid it was going to give way, so I dropped back to the ground fast.

Me and Mae were searching for four-leaf clovers when we heard Tommy. First came a shout, then a thud, and after that a strangled sound, like a cat meowing under water. Tommy was lying on the ground, his body twisted into a strange shape. The ladder lay next to him. At first I thought he was being his usual stupid self, but then he started to cry.

"*Tommy!*" I screamed, running to get to him. I pushed the tall grass away from his face, then ran harder than ever, straight to the Parkers'. My flipflops yelled at me, *fas-ter, fas-ter, fas-ter, fas-ter*. Across the yards, up the sidewalk. I slammed through the Parkers' screen door.

Mrs. Parker had scolding on her mind, but when she saw my face her words shriveled.

"Tommy," I gasped. "Something's wrong with Tommy."

Mrs. Parker grabbed the phone and dialed 911. Almost immediately I could hear the siren at the firehouse down the street begin to blare. It was a terrible sound. *That siren could wake the dead*, Mama liked to say.

The Parkers and I ran back to my house, where Mae crouched next to Tommy, holding his hand. The ambulance rolled up a minute later, and the paramedics jumped out with their fancy boxes of medicine.

We watched the men strap Tommy's head and neck to

a stiff white board. They kept warning him not to move a muscle. Mrs. Parker knelt on the ground, sobbing and crying his name. Mr. Parker watched. Every now and then he turned toward me and Mae, his eyes dark and accusing.

When they loaded Tommy into the ambulance, Mrs. Parker followed him in.

Tommy was silent the whole time. That was the scariest part.

22 The Hospital

Mae and I pedaled like our feet were on fire. When we got to the hospital, the ambulance was still out front. We knew it was empty but peeked in the back windows anyway. There was no sign of Tommy.

I led Mae to the waiting room, and we went to the end of the line of people wanting to talk to the nurse. Everyone had questions she couldn't answer. She'd type into her computer and then make a call. We'd hear "Uh-huh," "Okay," and "That's what I told them," and then she'd hang up and explain whatever it was to the person in line.

I kept leaning around, counting the people in front of us and reporting back to Mae. Five more to go. Two more. Then at last we were the first in line.

"We need to find Tommy Parker," I said. My words came out in a jumbled rush. The nurse stared at me like we were standing at the Tower of Babel and I was speaking in tongues.

"To see if he's all right," said Mae. She smiled and the nurse began typing.

I wiped my sweaty palms on my shorts.

The nurse kept pecking at the computer keyboard. "How are you related?" she asked.

"Oh, *we're* not relatives," I said, each word crystal clear. "We're his friends." There was more typing. "We were with him when we fell." I figured that had to matter. The doctors might have important questions for us.

The nurse gave us an impatient smile. "Girls, Tommy Parker is being well taken care of. Only immediate family is allowed into the emergency room. I suggest you go on home. It could be a while."

I felt my face droop. At that moment I bet I looked more pitiful than those sad-eyed dog piggy banks. The kind Miss Carmine had out front to collect money for the SPCA.

"But…," I said.

She shook her head. "There are no exceptions. Next!"

I plunked down in the back corner near a stack of magazines. "Stupid rule," I said to Mae, grabbing a few issues without even reading the covers.

"What now?" Mae asked. She sank into the seat next to me. Our eyes swept across the room. Rows of chairs facing the muted television. Hushed conversations between family members. Worried faces everywhere.

I stood and grabbed Mae's hand. "Let's go see Mama."

As we walked down the hall, I avoided the lines between the tiles, my feet crisscrossing to step directly in the middle of each square.

There was a visiting room on the third floor. The hospital kept it stocked with snacks, and usually there was a pot of hot coffee too. Sometimes it was thick and black, as if had been on the warming plate all day. When that happened I poured it out in the sink and brewed a new pot. I didn't drink coffee, but the smell reminded me of CJ's Diner and Sunday mornings hanging out at the counter while Mama worked.

At CJ's, customers blurted out "Coffee!" first thing, without even opening the menu. As if that was all they could manage before they had a sip. Once Mama brought a pot and poured the dark liquid into their waiting cup, they'd swirl in cream, maybe sugar, then grab the handle. Their other hand cradled the rim, feeling the warmth through the porcelain. They'd breathe in the steam and take a drink, and I could see the lines disappear from their forehead and the tightness in their shoulders loosen. In no time they'd be chatting away at Mama, telling stories about their week, eating their eggs, and using toast to soak up the broken yolk.

When we passed the visiting room it was full, people huddled in bunches of two and three, crying with arms wrapped around one another. A gray-haired grandma walked around with a box of tissues, pulling a few out and handing them to everyone. Preacher Jenkins was there too, Bible in hand.

I didn't mean to eavesdrop, but I could hear people consoling each other. "She's with the angels now," said one. "Her body just wasn't as strong as her spirit," said another.

The preacher nodded when he saw us. We kept walking.

If anything ever happened to Mama I wouldn't have a roomful of relatives to hand me tissues. It would be me and Mae and the preacher. He came for everyone.

When we got to Mama's room, Mae hesitated by the door like she was expecting Mama to sit up and give her permission to come in. "The day's a-wasting," I said, waving a hand for her to follow.

Mae sat on the edge of her chair and stared at Mama. "Can she hear us?" she whispered.

"I'm not sure," I said. "Part of me hopes she can, but another part hopes not. I've told her stuff that might get me in trouble if she wakes up and remembers."

We flipped through magazines a while, neither of us talking. I'd glance at the pictures, skim a few words, move my eyes to Mama, then to Mae, then to the hallway. Then I'd turn the page and start over. By the looks of it, Mae was doing the same thing.

I leaned forward, my elbows on my knees. "Think Tommy's going to be okay?"

Mae chewed on a thumbnail. Her shoulders hunched up slowly and there was a question in her eyes.

"Maybe Tommy was right all along," I said. "Maybe I am bad luck. First Mama, now Tommy. If anything happens to you, I'm leaving town." I gave her a weak smile.

We went back to our magazines then. I stopped at a picture toward the back. The summer sun shone down on a picnic, three generations filling up wooden tables covered with red-checked cloths.

"Is this what your family reunions are like?" I asked Mae, holding the pages open so she could see.

"I guess," she said, "except louder and messier. There are always kids running around and parents yelling at them. My uncles are usually telling stories we've all heard a million times. And then there's my mom! She couldn't be quiet to save her life."

Before I turned the page I ran my hand over that picnic, my fingers touching each of the smiling faces.

When Mrs. Parker walked into the room, Mae and I were half paying attention to some ancient black-and-white movie we'd found on Channel 2.

"How's Tommy?" we asked at the same time, both of us jumping from our seats to greet her.

Mrs. Parker gave us a quick squeeze. "The nurses told me you were here waiting."

She ran a hand through her hair and yawned. "Mind if I sit? It's been a long day."

Mae and I leaned against Mama's bed. "So Tommy's okay?" Mae asked.

Mrs. Parker nodded. "Tommy's going to be fine. Broke his leg, which they still have to put in a cast. The doctors are going to keep him a day or two for observation and a few more tests, but they don't expect to find anything."

"Finally we can go see him!" I said. "The nurses wouldn't even tell us how he was when we got here."

"Oh," said Mrs. Parker, frowning. "I don't think that's a good idea."

"But we've been waiting up here forever," said Mae.

I stared at Mrs. Parker, trying to read her eyes. "Why can't we visit? Isn't he downstairs?"

Mrs. Parker sighed. "Girls, I know Tommy would love to see you. But Jack is fit to be tied."

I jerked my head toward Mae and then Mrs. Parker. "He's upset with *us*?" The question came out louder than I'd intended. "It wasn't *our* fault Tommy was on the roof!"

"That's right," said Mae, nodding her head.

"We were the ones saying it was a bad idea."

"What was Tommy doing up there anyway?" Mrs. Parker said it as if it had been me dragging the ladder halfway across Tucker's Ferry and setting it against the house.

"He wanted to take a better look at that hole," said Mae. "We told him not to."

With a deep breath I squared my shoulders and raised my chin. "It wasn't our fault," I said again, each word clear as a bell.

23 Rosalea

Since Mrs. Parker had no intention of leaving the hospital, or not for long anyway, until Tommy was released, she'd called on Miss Martha to run the house. She didn't want me and Mr. Parker to starve to death while she was gone. Mr. Parker couldn't boil an egg if there was a pot of water already bubbling on the stove in front of him.

I listened to Miss Martha's small steps in the hall and down the stairs, the knotted wood barely creaking. Then came the faint sound of violins playing classical music on the radio, and the little noises of Miss Martha in the kitchen, shutting cabinet doors as quiet as she could.

Mr. Parker was up and out by the time I came downstairs. With just me and Miss Martha eating at the round table, the kitchen felt big as the school gym. I focused hard on the gray-brown oatmeal, counting raisins.

"Mr. Parker was angry yesterday," I said after a while.

Miss Martha shrugged. "Well, of course he was. Weren't you angry at that lightning? The fear of losing someone you love can turn people inside out." She stood then, took her bowl to the sink, and began rinsing, wiping it with a green and yellow sponge.

"Why, I remember after my husband died, I was so mad at him for leaving me I swear if he'd walked through the door I would have killed him myself."

"They might decide I'm bad luck," I said in between spoonfuls of mush that might as well have been cardboard. "What if they kick me out?" I had no place to go if they did that. No place but the hospital.

Her mouth twisted to one side as she shook her head. "Oh, Delia, the Parkers would do no such thing. My heavens, such a fuss over a broken leg. If you ask me, everyone's making a mountain out of a molehill. When I was a girl, every kid in school had a cast on an arm or leg at some point. Tommy will be home soon. Your mama too. The world will right itself in no time."

"How do you know?" I asked, my voice sharp. "How do you know everything will work out right?"

Miss Martha looked directly into my eyes. "I don't."

"What?" My heart skipped a beat.

"I don't know for sure," said Miss Martha. "But I believe it will."

"How long do you need to believe?"

Miss Martha stared out the window over the sink. "As long as it takes."

That afternoon I went to sit on the bank of the creek. The water washed over the stones, babbling and splashing as it rolled along. It almost sounded like it was talking to the frogs that were crouched in the grass, piping in a deep-throated *quark* every now and then. Birds were arguing all around, their voices loud and insistent.

I passed the spot where we picnicked, then walked on to the edge of the pool. We called it that even though it wasn't crystal blue with shiny tiles and a diving board. The water in it was dark as a moonless night. It was deep enough to stand in and formed a rough circle about twice as wide as the Parkers' grandfather clock.

There were flat stones near my feet on the bank. I picked up a few and skipped them across the water. The first one sank after just three skips, but I counted eight on the second one before it sank into the darkness. From somewhere in the distance there came the low, gentle hoot of an owl. It sounded like he was counting along with me, *two, two.*

Without even thinking about it, I took off my shoes and waded waist-deep into the cool. My skin broke out in a rash of goose pimples, and I shivered even though the air was hot. I plunged under the surface and spun slowly, my eyes open. There was nothing to see.

When I came up I struggled, pushing against the water to stay afloat. I tried to think light thoughts, but then I thought about Mama and the house and Tommy and my legs turned to stone.

I tried again, lying flat on the top as if I was going to make a snow angel. Arms and legs relaxed, I breathed deeply and let the water hold me up. With my face to the sky I shut my eyes, feeling the warm on one side and the cold dark on the other. Water seeped into my ears, popping as it replaced the air, closing out the world. Then it lapped over my belly and filled up my palms.

A bright, jangling noise cut through the quiet. I lifted my head and there was Rex, nose to the ground, stopping to sniff the trail and the weeds. In all my life I'd never seen Rex out of his fenced yard.

I sank down until the water was over my mouth. Then I inched toward a craggy rock, trying not to stir the water as I moved. Treading water, I waited.

Old Red wasn't but a minute behind, whistling a song I knew from Vacation Bible School. One of the ones with the silly hand motions. Rex's ears perked up each time he heard a high note.

I lifted a pinkie above the water to judge which way the wind was blowing. That dog would be on me like tar paper if he got a good whiff.

When I saw Old Red's cane land on the packed dirt, I held my breath. He hobbled behind it, his steps uneven as if his legs weren't exactly the same length. Rex sniffed at his pocket and Old Red stopped, leaning on the curved handle.

"Here you go, boy," he said, tossing a treat to the ground, then taking a seat o[...]orn wooden bench at the far side of the path. The ti[...]gged when he sat.

Rex cho[...] falling to the dirt. Then he wagged as if [...]dliest dog. You could have knocked me [...]on seed when he did that. As it was, I was [...]ter and trying to melt into the shadow cast by [...] and the weeds.

A fly buzzed past and perched on my nose. My eyes crossed as I stared at it and willed its tiny wings to start flapping. I tried wiggling my nose, but that fly stayed put, rubbing its gangly legs together and tickling me.

With a gulp I filled my lungs, then plunged to the bottom. Rocks and mud under my feet, I crossed my legs and sat there in the silence, wondering how long Old Red and Rex would stay. It didn't take long for my lungs to start screaming. I pushed off, rushing up through the blackness toward the murky light. My breath emptied out in one long stream of bubbles.

When the water drained from my ears the first thing I

heard was a snarl. There was Rex, guarding the bank like he owned it.

"Good afternoon, Delia," said Old Red, tipping his head as if he'd taken off a hat.

"Hi, Mr. Clancy," I said. I swam until my feet touched the bottom, then stood and squeezed the wet from my curls. With arms outstretched, I balanced across the slick stones at the edge of the water, my clothes sticking to me like a second skin.

I gave Rex the evil eye. "He won't bite, will he?"

"Not today. He's already filled his quota for the week." Old Red sounded serious, but it was hard to tell.

He started whistling again as I lay on the bank. Rolling that simple Bible school melody over and over again. The sunshine warming my skin gave me a drowsy feeling, and I found myself singing along, starting the same melody a few beats after Old Red, my hands automatically moving along with the words.

When the song ended I lifted myself up, leaned back on my elbows, and squinted toward the bench. Rex was flat out in the shade, his tongue hanging out one side of his mouth, snoring.

"You know," said Old Red with a smile, "I used to pray every night after Rosalea died that I could sing that song with her one more time." He smacked his hands on his thighs. "Guess what?"

"What?" I said.

"I feel like I just did."

I shook my head. "I'm sure she would have sounded much better. My voice is terrible."

Old Red's belly shook as he laughed. "So was Rosalea's."

24 The Preacher

That Sunday I paid a lot of attention in church. Without Tommy there fidgeting next to me, leaning over and whispering, I had nothing to do but sing and sit and listen to Preacher Jenkins.

During his sermon the preacher said we were all letters. That God had written something special on each of us. Some people were birthday cards, meant to spread laughter and share smiles. Others were letters of comfort, good at listening to hardships or wiping away tears. I wondered what kind of letter I was.

We got to the prayer part of church and Preacher Jenkins ran through a list of people who all needed remembering. There were folks like Mama in the hospital who were hoping for a quick recovery. Others were mourning the loss of a loved one. When he finished, he stepped from out behind the wooden pulpit and moved to the center of the stage, smack in front of the choir.

"Does anyone have any other concerns or celebrations?" His eyes searched the room.

I couldn't help but look around.

Mrs. Grey raised her hand before she spoke. "I'd like to ask the congregation to pray for my sister Anne. She lives in Chattanooga. Going in for a hip replacement this week."

Preacher Jenkins pulled out a folded piece of paper and a small pencil and scribbled a quick note. I never thought about his black robe having pockets.

Then a man spoke, smoothing two long strands of snow-white hair over his head. I'd seen him in the post office before. He cleared his throat and tugged at the collar of his shirt.

"As of Thursday morning, I'm a great-grandpa." There were *oohs* and *aws* throughout the congregation. "My granddaughter Elizabeth, she's the one who always came to stay for a few weeks in the summer, had her first baby this week. A little boy. Named him Joseph. God willing, I'll get down there this month to see him."

"Well, she picked a good name, Joe," said the preacher. "You tell Elizabeth to bring that baby in next time she visits." He paused, then asked, "Anyone else?"

My heart was beating so strong I was sure even Mama could hear it. Voices swirled in my head. There was Miss Martha yelling with a steaming pot of pickles, Mrs. Parker laughing as she wobbled on my bike, and Mama telling me how strong the Burns women were. *Folks need to stand on their own two feet*, she'd say. I closed my eyes, and then I stood up.

When I opened my eyes, the entire church was staring at me.

"Delia, what would you like to share today?" asked Preacher Jenkins. He came down the three small steps from the stage to the floor.

I took a shaky breath, my eyes focused on the hymnal I'd just tucked behind a wooden slat in the pew in front of me. "Everyone knows my mama is in the hospital." My voice was much smaller than the preacher's. "No matter what I do or what I say, I can't get her to wake up."

Heads nodded all around.

"You see, right before that lightning struck, the county

inspector paid us a visit. He gave Mama a stack of papers with fixes for the house. Mae and Tommy and I were working on them, but most were too big for us."

I could see a few people in the front dab their eyes. Something about that made my own eyes start to water.

"Tommy fell off my roof because he was aiming to fix the hole from the lightning."

The hymnal in front of me blurred. I blinked, trying to hold back the tears. Then I held my hands out in front of me. They were marked by cuts and bruises from ivy and saws and misdirected hammers.

"My mama would say that God gave us two hands so we could work twice as hard, but…" I looked around the church. Then I swallowed hard.

"I need help."

My mouth felt dry. No more words would come, so I sat back down in the hard wooden pew. Miss Martha patted my hand.

Preacher Jenkins strode down the aisle until he stood at the center of the sanctuary. Every eye followed him. "Thank you, Delia." I was wiping away tears but I saw him nod in my direction.

The church was quiet as a cemetery. I wasn't sure what would happen next.

Preacher Jenkins signaled the choir, and they began singing low and deep. "Now, Sister Delia is surely in need of our hands and our hammers," he said.

Most folks had their eyes downcast, as if they were reading a book. Like they were trying to hide from the preacher.

"Who among you will stand up and be counted?"

My heart clenched tight as a knot. With all my might I prayed for Tommy and Mama to come home safe and sound.

The preacher moved up and down the center aisle. The air stirred as he passed, his steps hard and purposeful. He kept his eyes up and his hands clasped together.

Then a single voice came from the back, loud and strong. "I can help," said Old Red.

Miss Martha leaned toward me as she stood. "Whatever you need, Delia, you can always count on me."

"Hallelujah!" cried Preacher Jenkins.

He scanned the sanctuary, a single question in his eyes.

Mae and her mom stood. And Mr. Pete from the hardware store. Sarah stood too, along with the Thread-Bears, who were scattered among the crowd.

A wave of *Praise the Lord!* and *Amen!* rose up from the congregation.

As I watched, one by one, every person in every pew stood up.

Preacher Jenkins walked down the aisle, his black robe swinging. "Sister Delia cried out in the darkness!"

The crowd nodded, murmuring agreement, watching his every step.

"And we have offered her a light." The preacher's voice was like an engine revving, filling the church with a powerful spirit. When he got to the back, the ushers opened the arched doors, and sunlight streamed in. I blinked, staring into the bright white.

"Were those just words?"

A few voices answered, "No, preacher."

"Empty promises?"

This time more voices called out, "No, preacher!"

The preacher smiled. "Well then, let's get going!"

He turned and disappeared down the steps. The choir left their spot up front in two neat rows and followed right behind. They'd shifted to a rejoicing kind of music, their voices bright. They swayed and clapped as they walked. Row by row, at the usher's signal, the pews emptied, people walking straight through the double doors, like we did this every Sunday in the middle of service.

25 A Billion Stitches

"Can we go any faster?" I asked Miss Martha as we drove home. I wanted to get started before the congregation arrived. It would take folks a while to get changed out of their Sunday best and get ready for working.

I stared long and hard at my house, at the sagging roof and loose bricks. I didn't see how we'd ever be able to finish on time, even with folks from church pitching in. My last hope was that the inspector would grade like the teachers at school. Give partial credit for things that were half done.

We'd have to keep working to find out.

With long rubber gloves reaching almost to our elbows, Mae and I scrubbed away that firehouse foam in the upstairs hallway, filling bucket after bucket of warm water. One good thing about the hole in the roof was that even with the milky plastic, the hall was sunnier than usual. The walls dried quick.

Then we tackled the loose moldings around the windows, gluing them in place and hammering skinny nails on the ends, to be certain they stayed put. We folded clothes, threw away papers, and found homes for all the little odds and ends I'd tossed out of drawers while I was searching for family pictures.

"Think Mrs. Parker would approve?" I asked when we could finally see the floor.

Mae stood there, tapping a finger on her cheek, scanning every inch, then nodded. "She'd want to vacuum."

We didn't have a chance to pull out the sweeper because Miss Martha started screaming at the top of her lungs. "Girls!"

We ran down the steps and headed outside. There, coming down the road like they were the high school marching band, was the congregation. I'm not sure Tucker's Ferry had ever seen such a sight. Walking together in a big group, toolbelts strapped to their waists, hammers in hand. Some held paintbrushes, others had shovels. I could see a few of the Thread-Bears with wicker sewing baskets hooked onto their elbows. The little ones didn't have anything to carry, but they skipped and hopped, keeping up with the rest. Three pickup trucks, their lights flashing, drove slowly behind. They looked like the cavalry.

Right in front, leading them all, was the preacher.

When everyone was gathered in the front yard, it was as if I'd forgotten how to talk. My brain froze as I stared at all those people. Not much earlier they'd been all fancied up, singing songs in church, but now here they were, ready to get dirty.

"Delia," said Mr. Pete, "let's see this list you've been talking about."

I led Mr. Pete inside. Several of the others came with him—ones with toolbelts who could probably miter corners, just like Tommy.

They huddled over the kitchen table, their heads almost touching in the center as they stared down at the papers. I could hear them talking, planning, deciding. Then they broke off in pairs and went back outside to gather supplies and rein-forcements.

"Mr. Pete," I said, stopping him after the others had left. "I've got some money here and I promise I'm good for the rest." I pulled the scrunched-up bills from my pocket.

Mr. Pete stroked his chin, thinking. "You know, Delia, there was a sale on paint this week, and most of what we've brought with us is left over from other projects, so I'm thinking five dollars should cover it."

I peeled off a five and we shook hands, like we were business partners.

When I walked back outside, a folding table had been set up in the shade of the oak. There was already a small radio on one corner. A gray-haired woman I'd met at the quilting club fiddled with the silver antennae. I caught her eye and she smiled. "The Thread-Bears do *not* work without country music," she said.

"We also do not work without sustenance!" called another woman as she crossed the yard. In her hands were two Tupperware containers. The good ones with tall domes to cover homemade frosted cakes. Except these didn't have cakes. They contained mounds and mounds of cookies.

Well, you'd have thought we yelled out *"Free money!"* when we pulled off the lids. The little kids came first, grabbing fistfuls of whatever they could reach. The grownups weren't far behind. I took a chocolate chip. It tasted even better than it looked.

Into my house went ladders, long wooden beams, all manner of screws and nails, wire to fix the electricity, and large creamy boards that Mr. Pete called sheetrock. Folks carried paint cans and white plastic buckets that, as it turned out, had a special paste for patching small cracks and holes. We had lots of those.

Mae and I were sitting on the porch, getting started on all those torn window screens, when we heard the sound of a car crunching down the road. There was Tommy, waving like a wild man from the back seat, making sure we saw him.

I cleared those porch steps in a single jump, Mae pinned to my back.

We bounced on our toes as we waited for the Parkers. Tommy struggled to get out of the back seat, dragging that white leg like it was a block of concrete. He moved slower than cold honey.

By the time all three of the Parkers were out of the car, it wasn't just me and Mae waiting there to greet them. Mr. and Mrs. Parker stood there, staring at the group from church, their mouths hanging open like they were waiting for a spoonful of cough syrup.

"Well, I'll be," said Mr. Parker. His face wasn't angry anymore.

"Welcome home!" said Preacher Jenkins. "How's the leg, Tommy?"

Tommy stood there, new crutches tucked under his arms, and smiled. "I'll be good as new in no time."

The preacher put his hand on Tommy's shoulder, and as if we'd been planning it all morning, everyone reached out to touch him. I held tight to his hand. Mae's hand rested on my shoulder and I could see Mr. Pete's hand on her shoulder. It didn't take long before we were all connected.

The beep of a car got us all moving again. There were two more folks pulling up in front of my house, which was becoming as popular as the Dollar Store during a half-off sale. Mr. Pete and the others strolled off to greet them and get back to work.

Mr. Parker cleared his throat. "What exactly is going on here?"

"You missed a few things during church today," the preacher said with a smile.

Mr. Parker grinned right back. "I can see that."

"Why don't we get some lemonade and I'll tell you all about it."

Mrs. Parker fussed over Tommy as he hobbled to the porch, directing him this way and that so he wouldn't fall. Mae and I kept getting in his way, even though we were trying not to.

As soon as Tommy was sitting down, we were all over him. Mae on one side, me on the other. Updating him on everything that had happened while he was gone.

"I bet we've sewn a billion stitches in those window screens today," said Mae.

I leaned over to Tommy, one hand cupped over the side of my mouth. "If we're up to a billion, then I've done nine hundred million of them. Mae is not going to win any sewing competitions." I added an exclamation point with my eyes.

Tommy grinned and shifted his cast, which already had colored scribbles running this way and that.

"Do I get to sign?" I asked.

I ran inside, taking the stairs to my room two at a time. A container of markers sat near my bed. I grabbed them all and ran back down.

"You first," I said to Mae, holding out a rainbow of choices. Mae pulled out red, blue, and a yellow-green that reminded me of those stinky towels at Carmine's. I tried not to stare as she wrote, but my eyes kept wandering back. In the end it said, *Tommy's cool! Love, Mae.* Overall it didn't look as bad as I thought it would.

I picked a deep purple to start, then took Mae's spot next to Tommy's leg. I ran my hand over the plaster, which was rougher than I expected. It took me a while to figure out what to write. When I finally started, my hands were a blur, grabbing color after color.

Tommy read it out loud once I'd finished. "Roses are red, violets are blue, roofs are trouble, and ladders too. Love, Delia." When he said the word *love*, it sounded a mile long, as if I'd covered his cast in lipstick smooches or a thousand x's and o's.

"I didn't write 'love,'" I protested, my face screwed up in a frown.

Tommy turned to me, his smile sugary sweet. "You drew a heart, and that equals love."

"Whatever."

26 More Vinegar

There were so many people moving around the house and the yard, getting in each other's way, it reminded me of the state fair.

Miss Martha was hunched over the back of her car, pulling something from the hatchback. "Take this, dear, will you?" She handed me a bag that was heavier than I expected.

I in turn handed it to Mae. "You carry this and I'll walk with Miss Martha."

"I do declare, I'm getting old," said Miss Martha as we made our way up the yard, her arm hooked into mine. Folding chairs had appeared from somewhere and now dotted the grass near the table, which was continuing to sprout food. Miss Martha plopped herself heavily into one of the seats and reached for a cookie.

"Oh, no!" said Mae as she pulled bottles and brushes from Miss Martha's bag.

"What is it?"

Mae gave me a face like she'd swallowed a cockroach. "More vinegar."

I turned to Miss Martha. "What do we need that for now?" Mae and I thought we were done with that foul smell for the rest of our lives.

Miss Martha popped the last bit of oatmeal raisin cookie in her mouth. She held up a single finger and chewed as fast as she could. "Girls, girls. Did you think vinegar was only good for pickles and windows? Well, let me tell you, it can shine up a floor like nobody's business." She glanced at all the food lying out. "Now, who wants to make me up a sandwich?"

Tommy and I left Mae to handle Miss Martha. We were halfway up the walk when Mr. Pete walked out. "Exactly who I was looking for," he said. "Need you to decide on a paint color. Come in and I'll show you what I brought."

Mr. Pete had three paint cans sitting in the kitchen, shiny dots of color on their lids. Tommy started talking before I even had a chance to open my mouth. "The yellow one. Delia's mama loves sunflowers."

Earlier that summer I never would have guessed that Tommy Parker was such a softie underneath all that mean and stupid.

"You're right," I said. "It's perfect."

After Mr. Pete and Tommy left I stood there for a minute, soaking in all the sounds. There were hammers and electric saws, talking and laughing, the distant twang of country songs and the crack of shingles being ripped off the roof.

When I walked back out to the lawn, the Thread-Bears had set up shop. Two more tables were arranged into a big workspace, with large bolts of fabric and small quilting squares all mixed together in the middle. A sewing machine sat perched on one corner, a long orange extension cord connecting it to the house. Tommy was there, leaning on his crutches as he watched the ladies decide on a pattern. They'd match up different colors, stand back and talk, and then shuffle them all over again.

"What did you decide to sew, Tommy?" A little teasing was good for him.

"*They're* making a cover for the couch. I'm just holding the pin cushion, is all."

"This young man is a mighty good assistant, bless his heart. And so handsome." The woman gave his cheek a pinch and Tommy blushed.

For some reason my own cheeks got warm too and I stared at my feet. I'd never once, not in all my life, thought about the words *Tommy* and *handsome* in the same sentence.

By the time Mrs. Parker showed up, Mae and I had been on our hands and knees for what seemed like hours, armed with coarse brushes, scrubbing every inch of the wood floor with a mixture of hot water and vinegar. It didn't smell as bad as a kitchen full of pickles, but it didn't smell good either.

"Oh my, that floor is brighter than a new penny," Mrs. Parker said. "Stand up for a second and let me get a photo of you. I might never see you working this hard again." She laughed at her own joke and we laughed too, at what a pitiful pair we were, half soaked with stinky water, our knees beet red from kneeling.

Mrs. Parker snapped shots of everyone at the house. I didn't have a camera, but I went with her, paying close attention every time she clicked, locking every picture in my head so I could tell Mama. Miss Martha stopped talking long enough to smile. Mr. Pete and his guys stood with their arms draped over one another's shoulders, an open box of doughnuts from Mrs. Grey half eaten on the table in front of them. There were pictures of the Thread-Bears, who were stitching by hand under the shade of the trees, the long fabric draped across all of them as they worked together to finish.

Out front, people I'd seen at church but didn't know by name were sanding the porch railings and fixing the lattice underneath. It had been hanging by a nail for years. One woman was even polishing the front porch light, standing on a stack of outdated phone books so she could reach. We took pictures of them too.

Old Red had arrived at some point without me even noticing. He was in the flowerbed, fussing with anything that bloomed, his wrinkled fingers stroking his chin. There were holes everywhere from his digging. Plants lay all over the place like forgotten toys.

He stared at the soil, then moved a few plants around, talking to them like children. "I don't think you want to be there, now do you. I suspect you'd like to be closer to the front. That way everyone can see you."

If I hadn't known better, I'd have thought he was one card short of a full deck. Tommy and I gave each other a high eyebrow.

"Pay attention now, you two," said Old Red. "We need to make sure these plants will play nice with each other. They're like kids in many ways. Some want loads of attention while others don't need much at all. There are tall ones and small ones too. If we don't plan right, the small ones will be stuck in the back and they'll be cranky the rest of their lives."

"Old Red, you've seen the swans, right?" I asked. "How do you expect we'll keep all *these* flowers from dying?"

Old Red gave me a wink. "You can do anything you put your mind to. And I've got my eye on those swans. We'll fix those weeds for good. You just wait."

Amid all the chatter, there was Mrs. Parker, her camera still clicking away.

I went in to wash my hands but stopped short inside the front door. Between the glossy wood floors, which must have been mopped after our vinegar bath, and the walls, which were now hole free, I could barely believe it was the same place.

I took a step into the room and ran my hand gently over one spot that Mr. Pete and his guys had patched. It was still soft and smooth as silk.

27 Transformation

I ran upstairs to where Mr. Pete was perched on a ladder, fixing to hang a new lamp in the hall. We'd never had a fancy lamp in the hall, and certainly not one with gold and glass. I paid Mr. Pete an extra four dollars for that. The old light bulb had hung by a limp wire. Which was a safety hazard, according to the county.

The new lamp would come in handy, now that there wasn't sunlight streaming in through the hole. I could see where Mr. Pete and his friends had put up a new piece of ceiling. The edges were damp and more light gray than white.

"We'll paint it once it dries," he said. "You won't even know it was there."

"It looks terrific just the way it is," I said. I meant every word.

Mr. Pete's friends were painting, rolling long strokes of sunshine onto the drab gray walls. The air smelled bitter, but it was way better than vinegar. I grabbed a brush from a tray on the floor and dipped it into the paint. The color wrapped around the bristles, finding its way between the strands. Miss Jackson would have been proud of me. I only used yellow and I stayed inside the lines, painting the edge of wall that the rollers couldn't get to.

"Delia!" called Tommy, a few minutes later.

As I ran downstairs, I could see through the picture window. Old Red had finished the flowerbeds and was waiting by his truck, which he'd moved right up to the end of the walk. He let down the tailgate. In back were pieces of wood, some longer than my arm, others about a foot across.

"Grab them all," he said, and he led us to the driveway. There were nails and hammers already lined up on a folding table, along with a drill, a brush, a can of white paint, and a chair for Tommy.

"What are we building?" asked Mae.

Old Red grinned. "As Rosalea used to say, 'A house without flower boxes is like a woman without jewelry.'"

There were materials for four flower boxes—two for each side of the front porch. Tommy worked on one. Old Red took another. Mae and I joined forces for the third. We struggled, even though there were twice as many hands to hold the bits together.

I hit Mae's finger only once, and it wasn't even very hard, but she cried out so loud you'd have thought I stabbed her in the eye.

Sometimes one hard smack was all Old Red needed to drive a nail all the way in. It took me about ten swings, even for a small nail. I didn't always hit them right, and sometimes they decided they wanted to slouch. What I needed was a nail with good posture.

"Feels good, doesn't it, Delia?" said Old Red, wiping the sweat from his brow.

"What feels good?" I asked.

"To be building something. It feels good to be building something again."

I promised myself then and there that I would put my mind to taking good care of every flower that Old Red planted. If Old Red could learn how to do it, then so could I.

"Come help!" cried one of the Thread-Bears. I ran over to where they'd been stitching and held out my arms, which were quickly loaded up with fabric.

"You made all this today?"

"This is only the half of it. Haven't you heard the sewing machine? We've been busy."

"Busy, busy!" said another woman.

My arms were so full I could barely tell where I was going as I climbed the porch steps. Inside, Sarah was directing traffic. I was certain she'd do fine in New York City.

"There you are, Delia. Bring those slipcovers over here." Other folks I recognized from church were rearranging the furniture, angling it this way and that.

I dropped the pile of fabric onto the couch. Sarah quickly sorted the different pieces, handing them off in drill-sergeant style. "Kitchen curtains! Grab a rod from over there. Table skirt number one! Slipcover! Who has the pillows?"

On and on she went, the pile of fabric dwindling and the room transforming in front of my very eyes. It couldn't have happened faster if Sarah had waved a magic wand. One minute there was ugly brown plaid and mismatched plastic; the next minute there were stripes and colors with pillows to match. It looked like a room I'd seen on the covers of those home magazines at the IGA.

"What did you do with the plastic tables?" I asked.

Sarah lifted the edge of a table skirt. Sure enough, there was the plastic. "Little designer secret," she whispered.

In the kitchen they'd added checked curtains and a matching tablecloth. As I walked through the rooms it was as if I was in someone else's house.

"What do you want me to do with this?" Sarah asked. She was standing in the doorway holding my Rainbow Jesus as if he had the plague. "It doesn't really match anything."

"Oh, we can't get rid of Jesus," I said, rubbing him on the head, then returning him to the table by the front door. "He's our good-luck charm."

"Heavens to Betsy, what is that?" Miss Martha appeared beside me, pointing at the yard. Coming up the walk were Miss Carmine, Mae's mom, and Preacher Jenkins, all of them carrying patio furniture.

"Delia!" squealed Mae's mom. "I won it in a sales contest! Isn't it fabulous?"

I had to admit, the wicker was just what I'd had in mind. "Thanks," I started to say, but Mae's mom was already off, cornering the Thread-Bears to tell them about the upcoming fall makeup trends.

That was when I noticed my swans perched proudly at the edge of the front steps. Somehow, while I was busy with everything else, they'd been reborn, their feathers washed white as snow, their black eyes repainted, bright red geraniums spilling from their backs. I ran out into the yard and threw my arms around Old Red, holding him as tight as I could. "Thank you," I whispered. "They're beautiful."

Old Red stood back, closed his left eye, and held up a thumb, the way painters do when eyeing a canvas. "They'll greet every visitor that comes calling."

"That's right," I said. "Every visitor." Mama and I never had much company, but I had a feeling that when she came home, it wouldn't be only the Jehovahs knocking on our door.

28 Fried chicken

Miss Martha had offered to cook dinner for all the volunteers, but she kept clucking about how much work it was going to be. Worried that she'd make herself dizzy with all that beating around the bush, I jumped right in and told her we'd love to help. Plus I wanted to learn the secret recipe for her famous fried chicken.

In her kitchen, a metal washtub sat on the mustard-yellow linoleum, directly next to the table. The edge of a white trash bag stuck out from under the lid, reminding me of tissue paper. It was an odd place for a washtub.

"Where's the chicken?" I asked.

Miss Martha handed Tommy and Mae and me aprons from her pantry and pointed toward the table. "Why, right there, of course. Did you think we'd be pulling it directly from the icebox and tossing it in the fryer?" She mumbled as she grabbed bags, boxes, and spices from the cabinet. "You three have a lot to learn about fried chicken."

"Yuck," said Mae, staring at the sea of pale, dead chicken parts.

Even Tommy thought it was gross, which was saying something. "They look like they drowned. What are they floating in?"

"Brine, of course," said Miss Martha. "Now put on those aprons."

The strings went all around us and back again, so we tied

them in the front. I hoped I didn't look as goofy as Mae and Tommy.

"What's brine?" asked Mae.

"Salt water," said Miss Martha. "Any cook worth a pound of beans uses brines. Makes the meat tender and juicy. Now wash your hands and dive in. We need to get all this chicken onto these paper towels to drain."

I closed my eyes and shoved my hands into the icy water. Nubby skin touched my own, making me shiver. Soon my arms were dotted with herbs and spices as if I had a strange chicken pox. Mae picked up a wing by the tip and dropped it onto the table, her face tight and pruny. Once he got into it, Tommy didn't seem to mind the dead chicken at all. Even from his chair, with that peg-leg jutting out, he was grabbing big handfuls at a time, letting the brine drip off over the washtub, then arranging the pieces on the table.

After the brine came a buttermilk bath. The buttermilk was thicker than the regular milk Mama bought and had a tangy, sour smell to it. Once the chicken was covered in milk we dumped two pieces at a time into a brown paper bag that had cornmeal, flour, and so many herbs and spices that even Colonel Sanders would have been jealous. Miss Martha let each of us hold the bag and shake it like there was no tomorrow. While we did that, she put two cast-iron pans onto the gas stove and heated up the oil.

She scooped up big spoonfuls of something from a glass bowl next to the stove and added it to the pan, knocking the spoon on the side of the cast-iron. "Always add lard," she explained. "My grandmother taught me that, bless her soul. Makes the oil taste better."

We shook and coated and fried for what seemed like hours, stealing crunchy bits off the pieces of chicken as they came out of the fry pan, until, finally, there were mounds and mounds of crispy chicken stacked on two platters. Miss Martha covered each platter with a cloth napkin so thin I could almost see through it. Mae carried the platters outside one at a time to a small red wagon.

Tommy couldn't carry anything since his hands were full of crutches, so I pulled the wagons while Mae and Miss Martha brought jars of pickles and cold macaroni salad with peas, which was one of my favorites.

"This is starting to feel like an old-fashioned barn raising," said Miss Martha as we walked.

"What's a barn raising?" I asked.

"When I was little we had them all the time. Every bit of land around here was one farm after another. When a farmer needed a new barn, all the neighbors would come over and help build it."

"Why?" asked Mae.

"Back in those days, everyone treated each other like family, whether they were or not. A farmer certainly couldn't build a barn by himself, and he couldn't afford to pay anyone to do it, so the only way to get it done was to do it together," said Miss Martha.

"That sounds nice," I said.

"It was," said Miss Martha with a sigh. "Such a shame; most towns don't feel like that anymore. Today, though, in Tucker's Ferry it does."

I smiled and kept walking.

By the time we arrived at my house, tables and chairs

had been arranged on the grass, with paper plates and cups marking every seat. We arranged the secret-recipe chicken and all the fixings. As if we'd planned it, a car drove up at that exact moment, and out popped Miss Jackson with fresh biscuits and sweet tea. We had ourselves a picnic.

Without skipping a beat, Tommy, who had already taken a chair at the table, put two fingers in his mouth and whistled. It was almost as loud as the train.

At least two dozen people walked out of my house. Not everyone could fit at the table, so I ran around and filled plates and brought them to folks sitting on the porch, those standing in the front yard, and others who'd made themselves comfortable cross-legged in the grass.

It must have been a summer miracle, because the talking kept going all afternoon, and even as the sun went down and the fireflies began their show, people kept grabbing a nibble from that table, and somehow we had enough food for everyone, including seconds.

29 The Inspector

When I woke up the next morning, my stomach was hop-
scotching around and my legs itched to get moving. The radio was playing. Spoons and metal bowls clanged faster than
usual in the kitchen. Tommy was humming across the hall.

I think we were all anxious about finishing up the house on
time, because no one talked during breakfast. We devoured our
French toast and bacon and then all pitched in for the cleanup.
I washed. Tommy dried. Mrs. Parker ran a wet cloth over the
table, and Mr. Parker put away the juice and the condiments.
It was a world-class speed record for breakfast at the Parkers'.

Even though it was early, my house buzzed with life. Not
as many people as Sunday, but then again, some folks had
to get back to their normal work. Mr. Pete was on the roof,
leaning over and tapping here and there with his hammer.
Miss Martha was clipping ivy with garden scissors, rounding
out the edges of the beds. I could hear the Thread-Bears, their
music wafting through the open windows.

In the morning light the roof looked perfect. I stood back
in the grass and stared. No matter how I eyed it, I couldn't tell
which shingles were new and which had survived the storm.
Lightning was no match for this new roof.

I was so busy admiring the roof that I didn't even hear
Old Red pull up. After a quick good morning, he set to work
on the flower boxes. Mr. Parker pitched in too, positioning

them on the porch railing, taking exact measurements so they'd be perfectly even and matching on both sides, then screwing them in place, good and tight. Tommy kept piping up, telling them to move things left or right. It was killing him not to be able to help.

When the boxes were up, it was easy to imagine what they'd look like overflowing with blooms. The kind that reminded me of a sunset on a hot August night, when the sky looked like someone had painted it. Old Red must have read my mind, because when he pulled flowers from his truck, they were all shades of pink and purple.

Inside, I could barely believe my eyes. It was like a field of sunflowers had bloomed smack-dab on the walls in my living room. Mama was going to love it.

I ran my hand over the couch and the tables, then went over to window, remembering Sarah's face when she saw the curtains Mrs. Parker had hung up only a few days earlier. I was certain she was going to keel over. I hadn't given them much thought. Mrs. Parker had done her best, but it turned out she was a lot better at riding bikes than making curtains. I made Sarah leave them be, though. They weren't perfect, but they fit right in.

The new porch furniture was comfortable. Sitting on a plump cushion, a proud swan near my feet, with the sweet smell of flowers all around, I couldn't think of anything else I needed. But Mrs. Parker must have had other ideas, because she came marching across the yard with a large red-ribboned box in her arms. She strode up to the porch and sat next to me.

"I made you something," she said. "I wanted to give it to you, even though it isn't quite finished." She touched my hand.

"No matter what happens today, I'm so proud of you. We all are."

There were people everywhere, but at that moment it felt like we were alone. I pulled off the ribbon and the lid. It was a book.

I set it on my lap, then opened the black fabric cover. Mrs. Parker had made me a photo album. She had spots labeled for each of the pictures she'd taken. I flipped through the storm-gray pages, reading the words and remembering.

Mae and Delia with beet-red knees.

Old Red teaching Delia to plant.

Dancing with Sarah and the Thread-Bears.

The painters splattered with sunflower.

Delia and Mrs. Grey, the cream-filled doughnut queens.

Mr. Parker celebrates — the roof is fixed.

The cooks with Miss Martha and all that fried chicken!

Mrs. Parker had a special spot for everyone who had come to help.

"Thank you," I said, my voice quiet. I knew if I tried to say anything else my eyes would start leaking something fierce. I didn't have time to say anything anyway, because right then we heard the familiar sound of a car driving too fast down the gravel road.

It was the inspector.

Well, I bet he about had a heart attack when he saw how different the house looked. Somehow, when I wasn't paying any attention, my house had come alive. That spirit who had hightailed it out of town during the storm had found its way back and come home to Tucker's Ferry.

There were at least a dozen people, including me, standing

outside when that inspector made his way up the walk, taking his time with his armful of papers. Torturing us slow.

He glanced around, "I'm looking for Mrs. Burns."

I stepped forward. "Mrs. Burns is my mama. She's in the hospital. I'm her daughter, Delia."

There was a glint of recognition in his eyes.

"I fixed things up the best I could." I turned to include everyone else standing around the yard. "With help from my friends."

"Looks like you've gotten a lot done," he said. His eyes were softer than I remembered, and he didn't smirk even once.

"Almost everything on the list," added Tommy, before Mrs. Parker shushed him.

"Are you ready for me to conduct the inspection?" he asked, glancing down at me. I noticed there were two pens behind his left ear.

"I'm ready." My voice sounded more confident than I felt.

As the inspector walked toward the house, Old Red walked with him, like they were school chums. "Is your last name Hobson, by any chance?" asked Old Red. When the inspector nodded, Old Red clapped him on the back. "I used to know your daddy." Then they went inside.

We waited near eternity for him to walk out. When he did, the chatter stopped. All eyes were on the inspector as he jotted notes on his papers, moving pages from the middle to the top and shuffling them around.

He came down the steps and stood smack-dab in front of me. "Miss Delia Burns?" he said, as if that was a question.

"Yes."

His face was unreadable, his mouth not smiling or

frowning. "I've completed the inspection, and..."

I could hear everyone waiting, holding their breath.

"There are still a few things that need attention, which I've listed here."

At that moment I wanted to cry, or melt into the sidewalk. I forced myself to be still.

Suddenly his face unfroze. "But they're nothing that would prevent me from telling you that you've passed."

A cheer went up and my eyes filled with tears.

While the inspector signed the papers, Preacher Jenkins let out an *Amen* louder than any I'd heard at church on Sunday. There was so much talking and carrying on, people slapping each other on the shoulder and shaking hands, that I almost didn't hear the phone ringing.

I ran into the house, leapfrogging the steps, and picked it up.

Well, you could have knocked me over with an angel's wing when I heard the voice on the other end.

It was Mama.